DOES THE WORLD NEED ANOTHER HERO?

SHORT STORIES

GLORIA SANDERS-WILLIAMS

A Desire4Fire Publication

Las Vegas, Nevada

Gloria Sanders-Williams/A Desire4fire Publication
Las Vegas, Nevada
Http://www.Fantasy-Author.com
https://www.amazon.com/Gloria-Sanders-Williams/e/B004N6SWO8

Does the World Need Another Hero/ Shorts –
Gloria Sanders-Williams. – 2nd Ed.

TO STERLING

When all else in this world doesn't make sense, your acceptance of me with only a 'slight' raised brow allows me to wear the 'Rose-Colored Glasses' that empowers me – I am stronger because of it. Thank you. Mom.

PROVERBS 3

My son, forget not my law; but let thine heart keep my commandments. For the length of days, and long life, and peace, shall they add to thee. Let not mercy and truth forsake thee: bind them about thy neck; write them upon the table of thine heart: So shalt thou find favor and good understanding in the sight of God and man. Trust in the LORD with all thine heart, and lean not unto thine own understanding. In all thy ways acknowledge him, and he shall direct thy paths. Be not wise in thine own eyes: fear the LORD, and depart from evil. It shall be health to thy navel and marrow to thy bones. Honor the LORD with thy substance, and with the first fruits of all thine increase:
So, shall thy barns be filled with plenty, and thy presses shall burst out with new wine. My son, despise not the chastening of the LORD; neither be weary of his correction: For whom the LORD loveth he corrected; even as a father the son in whom he delighteth.

*No road can lead to a
'happy ending' unless
God has paved the way.

"EVEN IN A STORY OF FANTASY
THE 'STORY' MUST END,

*DESIRE4FIRE

When a 'Hero' is born, is a sense of ethics a given? Will they stay the course; purpose-driven? Is there an oath sworn, a pledge upon lips worn? Is there room for compromise as the hero rises?

Is that hero hell-bent with eyes raised to the skies? As the hero toils, will they reach the goal? What sets them apart? Is it their approach perception, a role ingrained? Never surrender and practice self-constraint to never weaken, never tire; the heart must never faint.

Does a hero falter, fall, get-up just to fall again? Does a hero believe in their heart of hearts; they will always win?

Are justice and truth buried deep in their souls? Does it surface when the need is dire?
How do they perfect their role? Does a hero's heart stay lit – remain afire?

When questions arise, how does a hero sustain courage? What do they use to inspire?
What fuels the will; quells the fear inside –
How does a hero counter doubt when it conspires? Does one hope; should one pray.
Will a hero appear and show the way? Can a hero defend at all costs when evil is near?
Is a hero's heart protected – uncontested.

Is a solid foundation of morality encased within? Is courage manifested and then quadrupled times ten? Is your resolve set in stone, colored in black and white? Is the determination grounded when it is a life-or-death fight?
What restores a hero's soul? Does a hero play the game? What advantage do you gain? What ground is covered? What mountain scaled? What ocean claimed?

How desperate is a hero's grind? When is the path undermined, overtaken, undertaken by the blind?

Can a hero be undaunted to remain tasked? Can a hero afford to be caught without the hero's mask? And, sword in hand be quick like lightning – strike.

Hero claim no reward – lighten that darkened shore. Ignite hope; dig deep, find that 'something' within your core; set the spark to set the hero worlds apart.

Define in action no words needed to sow a path No herald is necessary to define the craft No need to boast of glory. This hero stuff is in your DNA.

Hero holdfast, become bold.
Fight and fight – take the road. Even if it's the one least traveled the one, only a hero, can take. Give your all; then give it all – all over again.

Commit it all – unwavering to the last breath. Be that Hero – until there's nothing left.
Give your all; then give it all – all over again.
Commit it all – unfaltering to the last breath.
Be that Hero until – there's nothing left.
That is when the 'Hero' inside is born.
And when asked while placed on a pedestal when you've passed every test. Does the World Need Another Hero?
The Answer is a given – Hell Yes.
Desire4Fire©2017

CONTENTS

DEDICATION

SCRIPTURE

POEM

LET'S PLAY A GAME   1

THE CATALYST   24

IN SYNC   38

THE ONE   47

THE FALL   59

BONUS FEATURE

THE DRAGON SHIFTER   70

LET'S PLAY A GAME

The two-story home was quaint with its stained-glass window that could be seen from the street that decorated the second-floor landing.

Its yard was meticulously landscaped, and the white stucco structure was the pride of the neighborhood watch. All homes should be modeled after this home and the family that occupied it.

Joy and happiness had lived there once but no longer.

Moonlight shone through the stained-glass window creating a polished wooden path. The flight of steps gleamed mahogany that squeaked when small bare feet ascended them.

At the landing, Harmony froze. Her trembling fingers, the color of smokey almond, grabbed hold of the railing; her other hand fisted her sky blue pj's until her knuckles turned almost white.

Harmony's hair resembled spiral curls that sprung out in every direction in disarray like an unrestrained sunburst. Her eyes resembled darkened storm clouds of gray. Harmony had been crying.

Harmony's face was perfectly round, not because she overindulged in her favorite sweets, but her genes insisted that she carry a little more meat on her bones.

One foot moved forward as the other that hadn't felt as cumbersome followed while Harmony's limbs trembled like jelly, but she managed somehow.

Harmony sucked in air as her tiny teeth pulled at the bottom of her plump lower lip before parting to exhale. She marveled only for a moment as puffs like dragon's breath escaped into the atmosphere before her.

Harmony's eyes focused on her destination; the door was right in front of her before she knew it. With trembling fingers, she reached into the pocket of her pj's and caressed the object that would secure her desire.

Her other hand grasped the cold brass doorknob, turned it, but paused. Her hand shook, but she steeled her resolve and pushed.

The room was orderly but unused. It wasn't quite empty either. Unadorned walls lacked personality, but it hadn't always been the case as Harmony's gaze fell upon the stacks of framed posters that lay against the wall abandoned in a corner featuring BTS, her sister's favorite boy band, and Usher, an R&B male singer her sister loved to listen to.

Harmony could almost hear her sister's voice singing 'Spring Day,' it was impossible not to sing it in her head now that she saw the posters again.

She felt braver, too, encouraged that she had managed to make it so far into the room without crying again.

Harmony also felt encouraged that she hadn't encountered anything out of the ordinary and walked further into the room,

She looked down as the fuzziness of a dark pink area rug tickled her toes. How many times had she felt the soft fuzz beneath her feet and wished her room had the same rug?

Harmony shook herself. She had come here for a reason as her eyes took in the twin-sized metal canopy bed painted white with pink covers that rested against the farthest corner of the room.

The drapes were drawn and intensified the gloom. Nothing seemed touched. Nothing conveyed what the Harmony had recalled had been her favorite place to visit.

She hadn't forgotten that 'happiness' lived here once either.

In contrast, the white desk with its three items strewn haphazardly on its surface tied together what had been missing.

Two hair ties, a pink girly brush, and a black book with the title 'My Diary' in golden filigree printed on the cover lay in wait for the return of someone that might have use of them.

Harmony's eyes settled on the last item that drew her attention, an empty chair. It was tucked into the grove of the desk. It hadn't been moved since that night.

She braced herself as her eyes flew toward the door and wavered for only a moment. Harmony was determined to see this through to the end; she hadn't brought the item with her to simply give up now.

It was cold, impossibly so, but Harmony could have sworn that the temperature dropped even more because her pj's tawdry material was a joke against the cold that swept through the room.

And, with the cold came a strange light; fear rose before her and shook her, but she hadn't come this far to run screaming into the night because she felt she should.

Instead, she focused on the air that shimmered in light and shadows.

Glowing eyes appeared first, and then a hand that reached out of the shadows materialled into the creature before her. It was then that he spoke her name.

"Hello, Harmony," he said.

Harmony heard him just fine but hadn't returned his greeting. As intimidating as he sounded, she felt incredibly fragile, her small statue against the grandeur of his presence, but she had something he wanted.

The rumors weren't right either. That if Harmony looked into his eyes, she would drop lifeless to the ground. She hadn't. Harmony was still breathing.

He had already given her a glimpse, and like the sun, his eyes were intense and full of beauty. They glowed, too, especially in the dark.

Harmony had been bold to seek him. She wondered would he vanish before he fulfilled her wish? And, although he knew her name, she was no longer afraid.

Harmony knew his name as well, or so she thought because he went by many names, but two had stuck in her mind.

Twirling her fingers, Harmony pulled the precious item from her PJ pocket and clutched it to her chest; she hadn't dare let it out of her sight.

It was also because she didn't know if she should let it go – her fingers tightened even more around the priceless metal.

"It's okay, Child. Hand it over," the Watcher commanded.

Harmony felt him a wretched being to ask her such a thing. Her opinion of him changed, and she viewed him with his careful eyes; he had wanted something too.

"You're her sister, right?" he asked.

Slow-motion took over time as the Watcher held out a bronzed hand as if the suggestion of his request were enough to make her comply.

"It's okay," the Watcher prompted, urging Harmony to hand over the item quickly.

"I don't think I should," Harmony said as her breath formed like frozen icicles.

It was as cold as Death itself, she had thought, but Harmony was determined; her mind made up. Her upper and lower teeth met in an unchoreographed chatter as her gaze followed her exhaled breath.

Harmony watched with innocent eyes as her breath rose on frost-driven wings, only to reform into ice and shatter as it crashed onto the wooden slats near her frozen toes.

"Then why are you here, Child?" the Watcher asked.

No question was more important, and Harmony's young mind struggled with the importance of her answer.

"I heard that you could grant wishes," she answered. Her voice grew steadily hoarse, but she had braved the room to meet the Spirit Watcher.

"No," the Watcher corrected Harmony, I grant only 'One Wish,' he whispered.

"Then, I have one wish," Harmony responded, whispering as well; her eyes blazed with determination.

The Watcher's amber gaze sparked with interest. "Oh?" he asked.

"I know that you won't grant it...my wish. Not unless I pay the fee," Harmony kept her voice low as her eyes fell to the object she held in her grasp.

Why were they whispering again?

Harmony had no idea; they were the only ones in the room. Still, she held on to the belief that she was doing the right thing.

She hadn't been frightened out of her wits when she addressed the Watcher/Spirit Shadow or whatever he was.

Especially since she felt driven way past that descriptor long before she had blatantly disregarded her inner voice not to seek him out.

6

She had only to give the Spirit Watcher what he desired to grant her wish. Harmony fingered the silver key as it gleamed in a light cast by something other than natural light.

She had stolen the object from her mother's jewelry box; it wasn't an ordinary key by any means.

Harmony took one final look at it before she exhaled, and more dragon's breath appeared to rise before her.

She hoped she wouldn't be punished for handing it over, but she hadn't thought it through past retrieving the key and coming here.

"Here," Harmony said as she handed over the precious metal; she felt little remorse in doing so. She had to do it if she wanted to see her sister Serenity again.

The room was pitch black, and as hard as she tried, Serenity couldn't see two hands in front of her. It weirded her out, too, because she had known that she wasn't alone.

The sound of his steady breathing gave him away. It had to be his eyes. Or maybe it was his silhouette. Either way, she had been certain – it was a man.

It was also that part of her that suggested she was a lot like her mom.

Magic flowed in their veins, and Serenity might have gotten a lot of her mom's discernment abilities too.

Serenity could do little things but never mastered any of what her mom tried to teach her. It was too late to feel sorry for herself in hindsight, though.

Some lessons took on more of a kick when common sense was delivered with bought sense. Because Serenity realized she had paid dearly for the not 'paying' attention part.

She squinted; the room hadn't grown any dimmer, but her eyes had adjusted. It was the same room she always ended up inside.

Serenity could mentally memorize every nook and cranny since she lived in this place whenever she closed her eyes at night.

Her dreams brought her here. They had started the same and ended the same with the strange guy watching her while she attempted to watch him right back.

Only that wasn't quite accurate either; Serenity could only ever make out his eyes. And, weirded out or not, she was stuck in the dream and never felt a reason to question it – until now.

It was only because she sensed his nearness like a sweltering presence inside her mind, but other than that, he didn't come any closer. It made her want to grind her teeth. Sometimes she imagined throwing something, but she had always been empty-handed.

Other times Serenity thought she might scream, '*Cut the lights on already!*' but that wouldn't get her anywhere. He never cut the lights on – it had been years already.

She had barely held on to her sense of time trapped for so long inside the dark. Still, Serenity was certain it had been a long, long time.

But, this night was different. Serenity hadn't felt so constricted; it felt like a window had been opened somewhere, and she could finally breathe.

Serenity's heart plummeted when she backed into something warm, and a hand shot out to steady her. Her heart jumped into her throat as she spun about in hopes that it was him. She'd finally get him to show her more than his eyes, even if he had just made her jump out of her skin.

Disappointment filtered into the deepest part of her as a pair of amber glowing orbs vanished. He was gone.

Those eyes had been watching Serenity for an awfully long time, but she was certain that whatever he was and whatever he wanted, he wasn't going to fill her in on why he wouldn't speak to her or show himself.

She wanted to pull her hair out; only she was certain it wouldn't help.

Serenity wished he'd turn the lights on or something – anything. The meeting in the dark was getting old. At least nothing had changed in the last three years.

Her senses flared up a warning. He had returned way too suddenly with something gleaming in his hand without light to embellish it.

Did he know how to use magic too?

When he moved forward, the gleaming metal grew brighter before it touched her hand. Serenity shrank away as if physically struck; whatever it was held magic – she felt it.

She had enough of his silence and needed answers.

"Can't you talk?" she asked.

She sought his eyes that were the only other thing she could make out in the dark; the object only illuminated his hand.

Then her eyes widened, and her heart jumped into her throat; she hadn't been expecting to actually 'feel' anything, but she had.

He had placed a thought inside her mind – a suggestion even. He wanted her to belong to him always.

Was he toying with her?

"That wasn't very funny," Serenity said as she stepped back only to find nothing to stand upon, only space.

She reached for his hand, but it was too late. Then the darkness swallowed her.

Serenity screamed, but the sound died in her throat as she fell bare bottom onto the uncarpeted floor from off her bed.

She looked up at the sound of laughter as gray eyes conveyed delight as they watched her big sister.

"Damn!" Serenity cursed.

Harmony continued to smile; pretty white teeth grinned on an even prettier face even if her eyes conveyed an emotion that Serenity just couldn't pinpoint.

"You're back!" Harmony said.

"Never left. And knock it off, Harmony; it's not funny," Serenity chided her sister as she crossed her legs at the ankle and rose before returning to her warm bed.

She pulled back the pink coverlet and sat with a huff.

Harmony nodded before she spoke. "You should thank me instead of fussing at me. You were having a nightmare."

Serenity nodded; she didn't disagree with her sister's assessment, even if her little sister wouldn't knock off the stupid grin from ear to ear.

"And I frigging wake up to you pulling me out of bed? Some sisters you are," Serenity retorted as she eyed Harmony.

Serenity squinted her eyes; something seemed different about Harmony. Had she grown taller?

"Can I tell you a secret?" Harmony asked as she sat beside her.

She was shivering. Serenity hadn't felt the cold but thought it strange that she hadn't since her breath formed before her to rise above her head.

Serenity shook her head and refocused on her little sister, who watched her with odd-colored eyes.

They were misty. Her little sister had been crying.

"Anything!" Serenity urged Harmony onward with the telling.

"Was it him again? I mean, the guy in your dream. I never got to ask you after you..." Harmony asked as she allowed her voice to trail off.

"Why aren't you laughing at me now?" Serenity asked.

She adjusted the covers and laid the end of it across her sister's shoulders.

"Was it him?" Harmony pressed.

Serenity sniffed, wanting to change the subject, and rubbed at her bottom.

"That hurt," she said, recalling her earlier clumsy fall out of bed.

"Tell me, please," Harmony begged again that Serenity share her dream.

"Alright. It was him," Serenity confessed and moved closer to Harmony to hold her hand.

"Was he in the dark? Did he appear creepy? Did you get a look at him, or was he beautiful?" Harmony made a funny face when she said 'beautiful,' and I wanted to punch her for making fun of me because of my highly suspect crushes on superfine boys.

"Funny. Least I know what good-looking looks like for a boy," I chimed at my little sister, whose questions had spilled out of her a hundred syllables a minute.

"I know what beautiful is too," Harmony pouted.

"Whoa, slow down," I managed, not even wanting to wrap my mind around my ten-year-old sister noticing boys.

"You're like ten years old; what do you even know about those things? Alright, yes. Don't forget the part that he had scary eyes that glowed this time," I said and hummed a tune like one that you'd hear in a scary movie.

"Wow, you suck at scaring folks," Harmony said.

"Yeah, well...who says I want to be an actress?" Serenity asked as she laughed and tickled Harmony's side.

She loved the way her little sister laughed – Harmony cracked her up.

They giggled some more before both grew silent while Harmony took a moment to gaze hero-worship-like into Serenity's face.

"Are you thinking about him now?" Harmony asked.

"Yeah," Serenity shook her head. "Tonight, he was different; somehow." She sighed into her reply, recalling her dream.

She leaned forward and rested her head on Harmony's shoulder; her sister seemed so sad.

Serenity even felt a little guilty because she hadn't even asked her what was wrong.

Harmony shivered, and Serenity watched her breath escape in cloud puffs before her – it was cold.

She drew the covers around them both as she spoke. "It's cold tonight."

Harmony looked at her big sister with gratitude as she pulled the covers around her tiny shoulders. "Do you want me to sleep in your room tonight?" she asked as she patted the pink blanket.

Serenity watched her sister closely; there was a definite change that had overcome her. And her eyes hadn't been dancing with its normal mischief either.

"Come on, Harmony. What's not funny anymore," Serenity asked.

"Do you promise not to laugh?" Harmony asked and tilted her head. She looked sideways at me.

"Cross my heart, and hope to die!" Serenity promised and made the sign of the cross over her heart.

Harmony winced but nodded. "I finally got to speak to him tonight. That's why I was in your room," Harmony whispered as she showed a dimple, but it hadn't stopped her from realizing how frightened her sister had been.

"What was his name?" Serenity asked. *Was it even possible for them to have the same dream of the same person?*

"He spoke to me. He said I had to pay the fee, and I did. He told me his name was Jayce," Harmony whispered.

"So, you got a good look at him? Was he tall? Was he dark with eyes full of light?" Serenity asked, her interest piqued.

The older sister felt something stir inside of her. Excitement? If they could 'dream share,' a possibility because of the magic they inherited, maybe they could build on a magical bond share together as well.

Their mom would want that. Serenity watched Harmony's eyes fill with uncertainty, though, or was it fear as tears streamed down her face.

"Not so funny now, is it?" Serenity asked and stroked her sister's back to calm her fears.

"I'm scared too sometimes, but then I can't imagine myself safer than when he's near," Serenity said as she came to terms with how she felt about Jayce.

Harmony looked up at her. "He wants to keep you always. What do we do?"

Serenity shook her head; she had felt that too coming from Jayce, but that had to be a misunderstanding.

"People don't 'keep' people," Serenity reasoned out as she smiled at her little sister.

Harmony had taken in her sister's words but still appeared wide-eyed at such a possibility. Serenity hadn't seen her this afraid in a long time.

Serenity couldn't imagine it. Harmony had more spunk and more smarts than the average ten-year-old.

"Want to play a game?" She asked her little sister out of the blue, determined to get Harmony's fear under control.

"Like what Mom taught us? Harmony asked as her eyes finally lit up.

"Yes, just like that," Serenity acknowledged.

"You'll be there the whole time?" Harmony asked.

"I won't leave you alone," Serenity promised.

"Do you remember how it's done?" Harmony asked, "It was so long ago...maybe we should ask mom?"

"Mom thinks we're asleep – which you should be. I was fifteen at the time, three years ago when I tried it before, remember?" Serenity laughed.

"I know, but it's unpre-dic-able,' Harmony tripped over saying the word.

Serenity laughed, "Yeah, I remember, and you'll be fine," she added.

She attempted to convey confidence in performing a gift rarely used. Would it be okay since their mom wasn't around to stop the game if she muffed it up?

Serenity was determined, though, failure wasn't an option, and Harmony needed her. "Ready?" she asked.

"Yes, let's do this," Harmony said with all the enthusiasm of a ten-year-old who was about to enter into a room full of fun and games, but what they were about to do wasn't any ordinary game.

The funny thing about dreams was that one was supposed to exhibit control over what was inside one's head. But there was nothing ordinary about Jayce.

He had been with Serenity for at least a few years; every time she had closed my eyes, he magically appeared.

Jayce never showed his face. Until he had spoken to Harmony. Serenity hadn't even known his name; she felt she should have at least asked him that much.

Jayce appeared just close enough so that she could sense his nearness, and then he distanced himself.

This night would be different. And both Harmony and Serenity would finally have answers.

Jayce had shown himself to Serenity's little sister, and then he had appeared magically before her too before she had tripped and fallen into the dark void.

Serenity wasn't about to let him get away with scaring Harmony or her.

Still, what she planned to do was a little frightening. It wasn't like she controlled Jayce's coming or going and, and she had no way to make him appear because she had wanted him to.

Her heart fluttered about inside her chest; it was more than just nerves. Serenity believed there was a connection between Jayce and her. He watched over her. She was certain.

And, she hadn't minded being trapped in the darkness as long as she knew he was near.

Serenity shook herself; she also felt clueless about why she agreed to bring Harmony along. 'Playing' with magic was dangerous, especially since she hadn't used her ability in such a long time.

Her eyes sought out her little sister; it hadn't felt right that Jayce would speak to Harmony and not her.

Was she jealous? She couldn't be, but she hadn't liked the fear he had placed inside Harmony's eyes either.

Maybe with Harmony's help, Serenity could manipulate the gift inside her to light up the perpetual darkness she faced every night. She wanted that.

The uneasy feeling inside her persisted, though. She had been crushing on a stranger she had never met. What if when she turned on the lights, she discovered that Jayce was a monster?

Serenity rapidly shook her head no. Jayce had been so much more than something evil in the darkness. He allowed her to feel safe inside a dream that she hadn't known how to escape.

Jayce had become her knight. Serenity shuddered. Or would he be her worst nightmare?

Regardless, she had to know. This night would be different. A turning point. All her questions would be answered. It was going to be an amazing adventure – it had to be.

"Sis?" Harmony asked and her big sister's hand.

Serenity squeezed right back before she swallowed the lump forming in her throat.

"It's okay, Sis," Serenity spoke in a whisper, realizing she had been too quiet.

"I'm here – I'm not afraid." Harmony's gray eyes pierced through the darkness as she gazed outward.

'But I am,' Serenity thought.

"Can you tell if he's here?" Harmony asked.

Serenity nodded. "I'll try and get his attention," she said as she scanned the darkness before her.

The room held a different feel to it. Serenity didn't know what to make of it. It felt magical, like a vast space of endless beauty inside a void encased in energy and obsidian.

And Jayce was close.

"You're here," she whispered as her breath formed before her as the temperature in the room dropped.

"She brought the key, Serenity, I'm sorry," Jayce spoke into the stillness of the room. And, for the first time, she knew what he sounded like – his voice was beautiful.

"I'm turning on the lights," Serenity explained. "Don't be afraid, okay?"

Something within her realized that her moment had arrived. She had never viewed Jayce in the light before; his image was shadows and haze inside her memory.

She only recalled the color of his eyes.

"Serenity, are you sure?" Harmony asked as she tugged on her sister's hand.

Serenity looked down, noting the worry that ceased her small features.

"Jayce won't harm us, will you," she asked the tall figure that had taken on a shape as he finally materialized out of the dark.

"No, I won't harm your sister," Jayce said. "I wanted to see who it was that loved you so much that it anchored you to this world."

"Anchors me?" Serenity repeated.

Jayce's words confused her. An uneasy feeling wrapped around Serenity – cold as ice.

"If you want to let go of your sister, then go ahead – turn on the lights," Jayce affirmed.

"What game are you playing, Jayce?" Serenity asked as she took a step back.

Jayce's eyes were mere luminous slits as he responded, "The same one your mother taught you."

"Serenity?" Harmony asked. Jayce had frightened her, and she grabbed frantically at her older sister's hand, "Let's just go."

"Don't let go," Serenity said instead as she turned to Jayce, furious at him for frightening Harmony.

"Do you want to play?" Jayce asked. His 'feel' grew even more ominous, and Serenity still hadn't made out his face in the shadows.

Even Jayce's eyes hadn't given him away.

Harmony swallowed. "She can't play anymore, can she?" she asked.

Her sister's words incited a warning inside of her. A twinge of fear followed to replace the bravado she once felt.

Who had she been attempting to fool? She sucked at games. She lost every time.

"Your move, Serenity." Jayce waited.

"You never called me by my name before," Serenity whispered as she tightened her grip over Harmony's hand.

"Turn the lights on – it's your choice," Jayce replied.

Serenity shook her head vehemently; she hadn't believed it for one moment. She had also grown suddenly fearful of the light.

Her knees wobbled, and her nightgown stuck to her back, soaked in sweat.

"We'll just go," Serenity offered. She also felt that she had been that close to begging as well.

"It's your dream," Jayce said but stepped closer as he spoke to us both.

"But it's Harmony's wish," he added.

Serenity blinked. Was he serious? She couldn't control what was happening if her life depended on it.

She felt when Jayce shifted his attention to her. "I've changed my mind. Your sister can go. I granted her wish – you stay," Jayce said.

"Serenity?" Harmony's voice shook with fear. Tears streamed down her face.

Serenity stepped forward without letting go of her sister's hand. "I can't do that. I promised my sister we'd play a game." Serenity said, forgetting her fear.

Serenity was pissed; her heart sped up to prove it. She hardly noticed when Harmony squeezed her hand again, but the warmth of it calmed her just a little.

Anger still sparked Serenity into action, though Jayce had some nerve to frighten Harmony; he had made her cry, and so she was going to make him pay.

Serenity would show him. She turned on the lights and blinked.

It took only a moment for her eyes to adjust, but what she had expected was nothing like the shock of her reality. The image of Jayce blanked any rational thought from Serenity's brain.

Harmony, on the other hand, had no difficulty in expressing what she had yet to acknowledge.

"You didn't have wings before. You're an Angel," she said.

Serenity's mouth dropped open; she just stood there and gawked at Jayce.

Humongous black wings folded behind his obscenely toned, bare torso. Jayce had flawless golden-brown skin, amber eyes, and the face of an 'angle' no pun.

Jayce was every teenage girl's fantasy; Serenity was certain because he was hers.

Serenity realized that she couldn't compare him to any of her previous crushes in all her eighteen years. Not in her lifetime.

"Are you kidding me?" Serenity eyes grew wide. She couldn't digest what was happening right before her eyes.

Jayce stared right back at Serenity. It was as if he were viewing her for the first time.

Serenity didn't remain unmoved; his stare evoked a strange feeling inside her as if all the blood in her veins had decided to rush to her head.

Serenity felt as if she was inside a toaster. Her body felt so flushed that she thought she might keel over and pass out.

Then another feeling hit Serenity as if she had just gone over a dip in the road in a fast-moving car – butterflies soared into flight, causing her to grab at her stomach.

Jayce winced. "I'm sorry, Serenity, I should have stopped you, but I wanted to view your face in the light too," Jayce apologized.

He stepped forward before he spoke again. "I think I will be severely punished for keeping you in the dark for so long, but I fell in love with you."

"Wha – wait...," Serenity stuttered. She felt tongue-tied. "This is just a dream, right?" she asked.

"If it were a dream, could you have turned on the lights?" Jayce responded in a calm tone because he must have sensed how freaked out she was.

Her gift was folding in on itself; she couldn't hold it together – too much was affecting her, and she felt her control unraveling like a spool of yarn.

"Can I leave now?" Serenity asked as she looked around for the exit.

Jayce shook his head as his gaze fell to Harmony, and he held up a key before he spoke to Harmony.

"Are you certain?" Jayce asked.

She didn't have time to answer him as her small hand became transparent within my own. She couldn't hold on.

"Serenity?" Harmony cried out.

Serenity couldn't stop what was happening as she watched her little sister fade to nothingness –

"It's too soon!" Harmony cried.

"Noooo –

Serenity scrambled to grab at Harmony's hand, but there wasn't anything tangible to grasp. Horror clutched at her heart. *What had she done?*

"It's okay, Serenity," Harmony's voice echoed into the lit room. "It was my one wish."

With no way to control the game, Harmony's form shimmered into thin air.

"She's disappeared?" Serenity whispered. "No – don't go," she cried, apologizing for losing control of my gift. For letting go.

Was Harmony gone? Just like that?

Serenity shook her head in denial. "It was all my fault," she whispered before anger snapped her into action as she wheeled on Jayce.

"You can't take her!" Serenity shouted.

"It was bound to happen," another voice filled the room and snapped Serenity's head about just in time to witness another strange figure materialize inside the room.

Serenity just wanted to stop the game and save Harmony.

"So, this was where you were hiding. If it weren't for the light just now, we would have never found you," the beautiful woman said.

And, go figure. She had wings too, but they were white, and she had curves to die for.

Serenity wasn't speechless but close. I

"Why take her? Take me instead," Serenity cried before she dropped to her knees to beg. She was completely devastated by what she had done.

"Silly, Serenity," the beautiful woman laughed. "Your sister is safe and sound. You're the one who has crossed over. You have been dead for three years. The 'Game' is over; it's time to go home now," she said.

"I can't be dead," Serenity argued, struggling to speak. Her mind couldn't register the women's words about her fate. The beautiful Angel was wrong, wasn't she?

"I'll watch over her! Please allow it?" Jayce asked as he knelt before the women in white.

"Jayce, if you take her – she will never go into the Light," the woman explained as her eyes bore into me.

Jayce rose and faced me before he spoke. "I can't leave her now," he pleaded.

The beautiful Angel in white regarded Serenity as she spoke. Then her gaze rested on the key that Jayce held in his possession.

"I see," she said. "You do have a choice, Serenity. But, it will seal your fate. I'm so sorry but, it seems Jayce has changed the 'Game.' It's far from being over," she explained.

"I... I have a choice?" Serenity asked.

When Serenity eyes sought out Jayce, he lowered his own. It was as if he had just recalled something dreadful because he whirled about almost in disbelief.

"She can't, Dara!" he whispered.

"You started this, Jayce. Now you must finish it; it's not too late for you," she paused and regarded me with a compassionate look.

"If you love this girl, do what's right for her – I can provide you with time," she said.

"How much time?" Jayce asked.

The Angel in white shook her head. "Not that much time, I'm afraid."

"Fine. I accept," Jayce agreed.

"Good luck, Brother."

"Thank you, Dara."

She nodded. "Where you go – I cannot know. Just don't run out of the time I give you," she said and vanished.

Jayce bowed his head toward the disappearing Angel he called Dara and turned to face Serenity. His eyes no longer blazed amber light but still reflected power and determination as he spoke.

"Are you ready, Serenity?" he asked.

She wasn't. She had no clue what had transpired, and she voiced her fear to prove it.

"I don't understand. I thought you said I must go home." *'Wherever' home was. It was apparently not heaven.'*

Jayce reached out and pulled her into his body. The butterflies started again as Serenity sucked in her breath; her eyes widened like saucers when his hands touched her waist.

Jayce held Serenity within the crux of his arms as enormous black wings flared out to lift them skyward with a care that belied his fierce gaze.

Serenity blinked with disbelief; they were no longer in the room.

"Am I going to hell?" She asked.

Jayce's eyes darkened as his wings engaged the space around them as he swept them both into the heart of darkness. He tightened his arm around Serenity; she had never felt so 'safe.'

Serenity's eyes strained to catch every part of his beautiful face before she shut them tight – Jayce had caught her staring.

"Serenity?" Jayce called.

She winced but kept her eyes closed. The beat of Jayce's steady wings made her reopen them as she watched his temple twitch in irritation.

Had she made him angry?

Jayce sighed. "There are far worse places than hell, Serenity. Only to go there means you can never leave – ever. It seems I'm to be given a chance to get this right."

Serenity nodded. Only, she held no idea what 'getting this right' meant to Jayce but felt she had the right to know.

"And, what is it that I must do? What will happen to me?" Serenity whispered.

"Don't be afraid. I'll be by your side, and I'll never let you go," Jayce said as he gave a reassuring smile.

"Okay," she said but felt all sorts of things tightened inside her as butterflies reappeared at the suggestion of his words.

"Jayce?" Serenity asked. She couldn't seem to stop the questions.

His eyes sought hers. "Yes, Serenity."

"What was my...choice?" she asked.

"You haven't been given one yet – soon," Jayce stated so quietly that I had almost missed his response.

"Where are we going," Serenity asked as lightning flickered within the growing darkness where Jayce carried her.

The reality of her situation moved Serenity to the point of tears – she had died.

Jayce squeezed her around her midsection as if to reassure her like he knew what she was thinking.

"It doesn't have to go the way Dara stated either," Jayce said as his eyes sought hers. "Serenity?"

"What is it?" she asked.

Jayce's eyes had returned to the glow Serenity had grown accustomed to for the last three years.

He seemed determined, and it encouraged her somewhat. She wasn't alone.

"Let's play a Game," he said.

THE END

THE CATALYST

The howling wind roared past me as I braced myself just inside the frame of the doorway.

The damage outside already showed signs of what was to come. In the distance, trees bent at odd angles, and debris scattered the whole of the countryside.

A pair of arms reached out to encircle my waist, raised me off the threshold, and turned me about in one fluid motion to carry me back inside the safety of my home.

The door slammed behind me. It hadn't drowned out the raging of the storm – it would only get worse.

"What do you think you're doing, Ash?" My friend's voice sounded close to my ear, and he placed me down next to a table in the kitchen.

"I just wanted to see," I explained.

It wasn't as if I could do anything more than watch anyways. It was a real pain – pretending everything would be okay when it wouldn't.

Plopping down onto the oversized kitchen chair, I allowed a huge sigh to escape my lips as I looked up to view if Savor would take the hint and stop eyeballing me.

"I'm not going anywhere – I already made up my mind." I protested. Savor watched me like a hawk.

"I know that you can be stubborn but, now is not the time, Ash," Savor reminded me.

I stared at him. He hadn't given in one inch as he returned a stare of his own with arms folded.

"If it's a fight you want – " I didn't finish as a loud crash caused me to react, and I hit the floor face down and covered my head and arms.

The whole house felt as if it shuddered as the wind blew full force, almost tearing the shutters off its hinges. Everything upended that wasn't nailed down.

I winced as the small vase that held my mother's favorite flower, yellow roses, toppled over. The vase hadn't broken, but water ran along the oak table's width and dripped over the edge.

I picked myself slowly off the floor, grasped the overturned chair, and took a seat.

Neither Savor nor I moved to clean up the spillage or set the vase in an upright position.

"Ash, please be reasonable," Savor asked as his eyes focused on what lay next to the overturned vase.

I can't help but look as well before I close my eyes and focus on a picture on the wall blown sideways, an oil painting portrait that depicts my grandmother in her youth.

'If only she were here. Did she know I would be left behind?'

"I'm waiting," Savor said as he reclosed the window and secured the shutters.

I ignored him still; my mood reflected the weather, stormy and unpredictable. I wanted to blame our situation on the weather but, I knew better. It wasn't the storm itself but what it represented that sent dread through me.

Neither Savor nor I had much time, and I hadn't concocted one idea to produce a doable plan; it was sad.

Savor watched me for a moment before he spoke. "You can make all the excuses you want, Ash but, it changes nothing – get this over with and go to the others."

"It's not like that," I replied. "Savor, you know what this storm means, don't you? You know I'm not strong enough to bring you with me, don't you?" I asked as my voice trailed off.

I had thought about several things, but the consequences were too great a chance to risk, and I felt the limitations of my powers immensely.

"It means we're running out of time, and you're stalling," Savor answered. He stood and then sat before he repeated his actions, unable to keep still.

I felt antsy too. "I'm just thinking about it – there's a difference," I said.

Watching Savor do something out of character hadn't made me feel any better, no matter that he had lost his cool.

Honestly? I had way too many important things on my mind to worry about my best friend losing it or not.

The fact that I realized I was in denial didn't help either. Savor believed in me; I was the one that didn't believe in myself.

Our world was falling apart before our very eyes because I had failed to utilize my magic to protect us. This was my fault.

"Prove me wrong, Ash," Savor said as his eyes searched mine.

"Huh?" I asked.

"Prove your plan will work – go. Do what you can, and if you find a way, I'll be here," he said.

'No, you won't.' I shook my head, no. I couldn't leave. I glanced up at my friend and felt the butterflies began.

Savor was handsome. His dark curly hair and deep dimples were what gave him his pretty-boy charm. And it worked; I was hooked.

He was also tall, lean, and with his athletic build, he could beat almost anyone twice his size in hand to hand or sword to sword combat if it came down to it.

I was certain that if Savor could perform magic, that he would have beaten me as well. And boy, had I wanted to fight instead of letting him have his way.

I glanced up, sorry when I had. Because Savor's eyes distracted me again. I think I enjoyed watching the hazel of his eyes change colors with his mood the most

I had it bad. I blinked, mesmerized, and not even knowing how he had managed to wrap me around his little finger.

Although, I hadn't minded the distraction because it allowed me time to be with him. I wanted to memorize every expression and tone that I could because I would have to leave if Savor had his way.

I wanted to memorize every expression and tone of his voice – I had to remember everything about him.

Savor was the epitome of the word selfless but, I didn't need that from him right now – I needed him to be selfish.

I wanted him to care about surviving when I had to leave.

"What are you thinking about?" his eyes search mine.

"Nothing that will persuade you to let me stay," I choked out, unable to hide the pain that seemed to hit me square in the chest.

Savor turned eighteen two months ago; he had always been my only crush, and it's obvious that I crushed on him, but he hadn't shown the same enthusiasm about returning my affections.

It hurt. I wasn't a girly girl and was a little 'tough' around the edges, but I had valued our friendship more than I could admit to Savor.

We had always been good friends, but I also wanted more. I didn't have a clue how to move that type of relationship forward without seeming desperate.

"Ash, how long have we known each other – since grade school, right? If you think you can keep this from me – you're way wrong." Savor confronted me.

"I'm not," I replied. "But, don't make me –" I glanced down at the object on the table and swallowed. "Don't make me take that," I begged, turning my head away from the offensive smell.

"I'm not making you do anything that you shouldn't have done already – we're out of time, Ash," Savor said, confronting me.

A bible verse entered my mind; bibles weren't kept in book forms anymore; they were considered antique pieces; no one read off paper anymore – everything was electronic, and billions of trees had been saved because of it.

This verse has always been with me, though; it's all things about Time.

Ecclesiastes: 3 in the Bible states: 'To everything, there is a season, and a time to every purpose under the heaven: A time to be born, and a time to die; a time to plant, and a time to pluck up that which is planted; a time to kill, and a time to heal; a time to break down, and a time to build up; a time to weep, and a time to laugh; a time to mourn, and a time to dance; a time to cast away stones, and a time to gather stones together; a time to embrace, and a time to refrain from embracing; a time to get, and a time to lose; a time to keep, and a time to cast away; a time to rend, and a time to sew; a time to keep silence, and a time to speak; a time to love, and a time to hate; a time of war, and a time of peace.

Time was my archnemesis. I had wanted to grasp it like it's a tangible thing but, I couldn't. I could only hold on to the scripture and hope that things worked out for the good of all things.

Time meant more to me than I thought possible, especially since I couldn't recreate it.

Something has occurred, the moment when 'Time' means everything – every precious second must account for something.

My magic is unique; I had even made the argument that no vessel that manipulates space or time should have such power to do so – there so much that can go wrong. I have also done something terrible. I'm certain those in control will attempt to discipline me, but I couldn't let well enough alone, and I certainly couldn't desert my closest friend. Not even my parents could shake my determination. Now, I've waited until I was the very last of my kind to leave, and in doing so – this world will whittle away at its core until nothing is left.

It takes every ounce of my strength to the point that drains me dry, and only with a medicinal cure can I recover but, the Mendolum Tree bark is difficult to acquire, and we tease that a person almost must sell their soul to obtain it. If I don't consume the tree bark, I can't regain my magic, and if I can't recover my magic, I can't join the others.

Those without the gift of magic will not be able to follow us to safety – the planet is dying.

The storm raged outside, a direct consequence of losing my magic. It was what crippled this world.

My best friend, Savor, expected me to join the others. The decision was over and done with about who would end up staying behind.

And, those who did took their chances on chance.

In the end, those who carried no magic, like Savor, were the casualties of a world bereft of magic – abandoned.

I hadn't wanted to accept that outcome. I couldn't admit it.

Savor deserved my help. Unfortunately, I had used up all my resources.

Somehow, I had believed that I had found the answer – using the last of my magic to stall the storm.

But, it had only drained me of my powers, while I had gained just a few months.

I was stuck as well.

"Why so quiet?" Savor squatted beside my chair and played with my hair to get my attention.

"Honestly?" I asked.

"Yeah?

"Have you ever tasted Mendolim bark?" I asked instead, changing the subject.

"Fine, Ash – I can't make you want to live," Savor rose and paced before me.

"I do want to live but, I want you to make it out too," my voice sounded whiney. To me, nothing seemed worse than loving someone and being unable to save that person.

I felt utterly helpless, and I just hadn't known how to express my uselessness.

Loving someone on a standalone basis would never be enough to save that individual from impending doom.

The most horrible part of acknowledging such a fact is the acquirement of one's fate beforehand.

I exhibited such a talent, and I was cursed – heartbroken because of it.

Savor leaned over me, "I wasn't aware such a pretty face could become so frumpy. You're going to get wrinkles," he teased.

I stuck my tongue out, "You can go suck rocks," I retorted back.

Savor ignored me.

He didn't push the point, but I could tell that he needed to make a decision soon.

He stole a glance my way to check my progress. His eyes lightened from intense green to an almost jade color; his smirk was as familiar as the rise of irritation it provoked.

Even though I didn't have enough energy to spearhead an argument, and I looked everywhere, but at Savor before I glanced back down at my plate.

I hadn't known what to say, regardless. I couldn't help but worry – did he sell his soul?

"Are you going to eat that?"

I looked up, startled out of my gloomy thoughts with a ready-made excuse as to why 'No, I wasn't going to Eat That.'

I took in a deep breath before exhaling and calmed my nerves. I was determined I get Savor to spill the beans as to how he had acquired the unobtainable.

"Sav?" I asked. I felt frightened that it would be worse than I feared.

So, I changed the subject with a direct answer to why I couldn't do what he asked.

"If I eat this stuff," I waved my hands at the offensive dark pieces of tree bark on my plate and made a face.

"I was going to throw up," I said.

That's right – tree bark, not steak or chicken; not even something edible.

"How am I supposed to want to eat this?" I asked and pointed at the disgusting bark.

"Ash, it'll help you regain your magic," Savor explained to me as one would a small child.

I don't think he would have eaten it himself regardless of his assertion that I could do it as if I should know why I must eat Mendolum bark in the first place.

The one true remedy known to aid people like me whose talents have gone dormant, Savor was right – eating the tree bark was the only way.

That and using a coveter's ring, which I didn't possess.

"The Others will be worried by now; they will wonder what's taking you so long," he said.

Savor was right about that too. It was my magic that must seal the portal to this world – I am the Catalyst. Time will no longer wait for me to decide

"And – if you throw it up, you'll have to start from scratch all over again," he said.

"It stinks," I covered my nose.

"It does but, it will still help you regain your powers."

"I hate my abilities," I whined.

"Says the girl who knows all – sees all," Savor said with a wink.

Tears stung my eyes – that was just it. I couldn't evade the truth much longer.

"When are you going to tell me?" Savor asked.

I blinked – I want to know things too.

Savor knew of my secret but, I wasn't privy to what he kept locked up inside his beautiful mind.

Even though I want to play 'dumb' a little longer, I tried to hold on to my simplistic version of reality for at least ten more minutes.

Why did Savor wish to end my happiness?

I also had no words, and a tear slid down my cheek.

"Tell you what? That you a pain in my backside?"

"Yes, if you want," Savor smiles at me; his patience is unending.

I hated to admit it, but I had wished I didn't say such mean things, especially when every precious moment in Savor's company meant the world to me.

'How much are you willing to sacrifice for a few moments more, Ash?'

I pretended I hadn't heard the voice that pleaded. I accepted Savor's offering to flee this place.

Instead, I wanted to remain like this always by Savor's side; it is my sincerest desire.

"Well, you're not a pain...not really," I managed to look into the eyes of my friend.

"I'll always be with you, Ash – here and here," he pointed at my forehead and next to my heart.

When I sighed, I realized I was never good at expressing my feelings, and any sarcasm seemed a waste of our last moments together.

"Stop acting like this didn't cost you more than you can afford to sacrifice," I said.

"Stop acting like it wasn't the same for you," Savor said.

He frowned for the first time since I could remember.

"I can't eat this stuff," I changed the subject and pushed the plate to the middle of the table.

Savor stood and pushed the plate back in front of me, "EAT."

"I CAN'T!" *'I can't...I can't.'*

I can't stop the tears. I can't control what was going to happen. I hated pain. I hated storms. I hated that I loved Savor and couldn't keep him safe.

And, while I was good at denial, Savor believed I was special. If he thought it, then so must I – right?

I looked at the plate and finally asked the question that bothers me, "How did you get it? You shouldn't have done this; there had to be another way to obtain the Mendolum. Is that why I can't bring you through with me?" I asked. I hadn't foreseen any of it. It just hadn't seemed fair.

"It doesn't matter, Ash. I won't be around to defend my actions, and you don't have to tell them anything – you won't have to lie on my behalf," Savor explained.

My eyes took in my friend. Savor almost had deduced me to tears by his brave words.

I was nothing like him.

He had already thought it through. My act of bravery compared to his seemed trivial.

We both did what we felt we had to do.

'No more stalling.' I glanced at the dark, broken pieces of tree bark and almost gagged.

There must be a way to save him after I'm gone – right?

I looked up at the boy I loved and found strength in his being close and courage in his willingness to be left behind.

Savor changed the subject and held out his hand, so I could see what he held in the palm of it, "Aren't you going to try it on?" he asked.

He had thought of everything.

In his grasp was a tarnished old gemstone ring for me to take.

I gulped down my fear and held out my hand, and nodded, "It's not like I'm afraid or anything."

My knees were shaking underneath the table to prove my bravado had been nothing but a façade.

The pounding in my chest also seemed unbearably loud.

I held my palm face upward to receive the old ring.

Savor smiled at me, "I meant to give you that for a while; it was something Nana left me. She said I would know what to do with it when the time was right – I guess that time is now," he said.

"I'm sorry about your grandmother," I said.

"I thought of you and wanted you to have it. Nana is gone but, she loved you too," he explained.

"Does it even fit?" I asked, sounding ungrateful.

I straightened up and attempted a smile, "Thanks," I added.

Savor wasn't giving me his grandmother's ring because he had feelings for me or anything.

At least not like the feelings that drowned me and overwhelmed me because I realized that I loved him.

"It should be okay – it molds to the wearer's finger, my grandmother told me; that is if the person is worthy to receive it," Savor guided the onyx ring onto my left ring finger – it fit.

"See! No worries," Savor said.

His dimpled smile made my heart melt. "Yea. It fits," I whispered.

"Hey! Don't sound so thrilled," Savor said.

"I am – " I shook my head as a ringing erupted in my ears.

"What did you say?" I asked Savor.

"I said it look good on you; it will serve you well." Savor looks pleased with himself, and I know I just look 'embarrassed.'

It felt incredibly warm and as sudden as the band tightened around my finger.

It had also begun to glow. What was once a tarnished band becomes shiny with rune markings inscribed. Afterward, the ring expands and is a perfect fit once more.

"What...what was that?" I jumped out of my seat.

In actuality, my mind is racing ahead, searching a world I've never seen, drawn into the center gemstone as my vision faded to black and then my sight returned intensified.

The vision lasted only a few moments before I dropped like a stone onto my seat.

I felt exhausted as if I had run several miles.

'This complicates matter but, what's done, is done.' I heard a voice say.

"What did you say?" I asked Savor.

"I said...now it should work if you just eat that," he jerked his head over to the plate, the bark still untouched by the likes of me.

"Your grandmother was a Quester, wasn't she?"

"Yes, but later she retired to Coveter."

"Like my mother," I said.

"Which with the help of this ring it will multiply your gift ten-fold. That's why I thought to have this might ease your worry," Savor takes my hand into his own, "You'll be able to find me anywhere."

"What?" I asked.

"You believe I don't care about you, don't you, Ash."

I snatched my hand out of his, "It's not like that." I said. "We're friends, right?"

"Yes. We're friends," Savor began. "But – I like us to be more."

Stunned into silence, I gazed into Savor's greens eyes that seemed to sparkle more than I had ever noticed before.

"Like...more than friends?" I stuttered.

"If you will have me?" Savor said as he held out his hand.

Tears stung my eyes. How could I abandon him now?

"Yes," I said.

"Then will you eat the Mendolum?" Savor lifted a small piece of the bark to my lips.

"This is evil bribery," I sniffed.

Savor laughed,

Before I could retort, he moved the bark aside and leaned in to touch his lips to my own.

And, with my first kiss, my mind went blank. When I could think again, all I wanted to do was remain in the moment alongside a boy that I liked more than anyone – loved more than anyone.

I wanted emotion to take me, but not like this; I felt as if I was drowning in sorrow and sweet bliss all at once.

Savor leaned back, watching me intently before he leaned in to kissed me again. His lips pressed tightly to mine, and I closed my eyes and went with it. I wanted to remember everything about that kiss.

Hot tears hit my cheek, and Savor released my lips to kiss softly where they fell.

"I'm afraid," I confessed.

"There's nothing to fear but fear itself. You're stronger than its ability to stop you from doing what is needed, Ash. I have faith in you," Savior whispered near my ear.

I reopened my eyes and sought the gaze of the boy I loved.

"We are together now?" he asked.

"Yes," I acknowledge our newly joined relationship and reached to place my hand on his cheek. "I want that more than anything," I said.

Savor smiled and kissed my hand before he squatted before me and placed the awful bark near my lips again.

I sighed and opened my mouth.

The bark tasted bitter as I nibbled off my first bite and chewed the tough texture that reminded me of defeat and pain as I made a face. It wasn't easy to swallow, but I managed.

"Now what?" I asked.

At that moment, it was as if my words of acceptance brought the ring to life.

I deciphered the inscription on the band as it flared in brilliance and warmed my finger in the process.

The black center stone becomes almost blue-black in clarity as I can now see the images form in its center.

"I love you, Ash. I always have – I promise you; I won't leave you – remember. But that means you have to find me. You're the daughter of a Coveter after all – right?" Savor asked.

His words placed me in despair as he pointed to my forehead and my heart, "I will always be here and here. Now go save this world," he commanded.

"What's happening?" I asked.

I knew I would treasure Savor's words, and I desired that he knew how I felt too.

Only, things don't unfold the way one would hope – just because.

Not in a world where magic dictates those who get to live and those who must be left behind only to live in one's heart and mind.

My magic couldn't save the boy I loved from having no magic of his own. His determination that I was gone before the Storm arrived reiterated that fact.

It was why I knew I loved him more than he loved me. His eyes informed me that deep down that I was incorrect about who loved who the deepest.

Savor loved me enough to want me to live.

"I love you, Ash," Savor said once more.

"Savor?" It was the only word that had time to escape my lips before the center stone lent me its power, and I left my world behind.

THE END

IN SYNC

For a moment, I had lost track of where I was; the air smelt stale – almost impossible to breathe.

I looked up from my stupor only to note two pair of eyes watching me intently. I had never seen more impatience in someone's eyes than I did at that moment.

"I'll just come back when you're ready," the waiter huffed.

"No, she'll have a cocktail. Make it a 'Sex-On-The-Beach', heavy on the Alize," my date ordered.

"I'm not certain I want something that strong," I held the eyes of the waiter and thought of a drink I'd prefer to counter my date's heavier choice – I didn't have one.

"She'll take what I ordered. I'll have a Scotch on the rocks." Alister brushed off the waiter as my boyfriend smiled back into my eyes.

"What was that all about?" I asked.

The waiter was about halfway down the aisle; I couldn't place if I had seen him before, but my memory seemed sketchy. Something was off.

And, I hung on to that uneasy feeling like a warm blanket when it felt cold outside.

"What's with the stare? You act as if you don't know what you're doing – you'll blow our cover," Alister gave me a worried look.

38

"Are we working?" I asked. I wasn't informed.

I figured this was a real date. My look must have been a dead give-away because Allister changed his body posture right before my eyes.

He settled into his part perfectly, his old 'lady- killer' self again. "It could be," he winked.

His sexy smirk was too much for me to take, and I snatched at my water glass to take a sip.

'Cool it, Steel,' I scolded myself. *'What was wrong with me?'*

The water tasted sweet, ice cold, but then I noticed the aftertaste as it hit my tongue.

Smiling up at Allister, I placed the water glass down without swallowing – that was close.

"You're going to fill me in?" I whispered as I took my first look around, noticing more than I wanted.

If the target was nearby, I hadn't a clue because the restaurant was jam-packed – it could be anyone.

"You catch on quick, Steel," Allister said. He always called me by my sir name; he didn't even acknowledge my given name – which was?

"They haven't arrived yet; I'll let you know when they show; just take my lead," Allister said.

"Shouldn't I be briefed?" I asked as I chewed on my bottom lip.

"Your eyes are gorgeous," Alister complimented me as he flirted. I also knew that he used that tactic when he wished to avoid a direct question.

I relaxed and smiled while attempting to figure out what was wrong.

For one thing, I was always able to tell when Allister was serious and when he wasn't, but I guessed that was what made us surprisingly good partners – our chemistry.

His eyes stayed on mine; I guess it worked both ways as something triggered a warning inside me – something wasn't right.

I no longer needed to figure out what that something had been. I couldn't sense my partner; Allister appeared a little too perfect with his smile, and his eyes seemed –

I leaned forward. My senses absorbed the nuisance of sounds that filtered around me as I 'melded.' I held the ability to go between space and time as I pulled in light so that I could truly see.

'What game am I playing?'

A noise got my attention; someone was attempting to connect with me and then realized who it was.

I decided the game was a little too high stakes to stay and play – I wasn't wrong.

"So – what happened between us the other night was?" I focused only on his eyes and not his response.

"Huh? Oh, that? It couldn't be avoided," Allister finished.

I sighed. "I guess that sort of leaves me no options," I replied as I turned my head to count precisely how many guns I would need to avoid.

The timing was everything; I waited for the waiter to make his way back to our table with our drinks.

'Now, Steele!' a voice directed me.

I'd recognize that voice anywhere, and with the exactness of my training, I whipped out my left leg and tripped the waiter.

It diverted him into the unsuspecting arms of Allister while I ducked to my left and avoided a knife thrown at point-blank range.

I yanked up my short dress to gain easy access to my thigh holster, drew my Glock, took aim, and got off six rounds – my aim perfect. Deadly.

I threw my body across the table to the other side of the aisle and emptied my weapon. I could have performed such a maneuver in my sleep. Besides, panic wasn't an option as I reached for my clip to reload.

More targets appeared than I was prepared to confront; two behind the bar and the man that sat left of our table, and with three clean shots, I took them out of the picture.

The Glock felt warm in my palm, like an old friend, and I

sighted any potential danger as I ran through the panicking patronage and ducked behind a wall that led to the kitchen galley.

'Don't Stop – two more!' the voice that entered my thoughts advised.

'Thanks!' I whispered, as I hurled my body forward in a duck and roll move before I rose and burst through the kitchen, pushing aside a cook who had just plated a Cornish Hen.

I rounded the corner on a dead run and scrambled for the back door before the plate hit the floor using the fleeing cooks as cover.

A reflection in the glass made me hit the deck, but I bounced up in less than a heartbeat as the bullet ricocheted off the metal frame of the back door.

I slammed my hand against the door bracket as it gave way and allowed me freedom as I bolted out the back door in an all-out sprint and down the alley.

I had hoped that my high heels didn't do me in because I wasn't going to take the chance to stop and take them off.

A flash in the distance that couldn't be seen without knowing what to look for indicated that I only needed five kelonio-meters to clear the exit point.

'Steel – left,' a voice sliced into my thoughts.

Damn! I turned left, still at an all-out sprint, and duck behind the huge robotic carriers used for garbage bins; one saved my life as it took on about twenty rounds from a semi-automatic weapon of destruction.

"What next?" I asked.

'Two K- meters to go,' the voice confirmed.

"Okay, I'm ready," I whispered, gearing up to make the extraction point or die trying.

'Not yet – on my mark. Thirteen degrees left, one shot – don't miss.'

"As if I ever," I stated the obvious.

I quieted my beating heart as I allowed air to fill my lungs; I slowly exhaled and aimed before squeezing the trigger.

"All clear," I said and ran like the demon hell hound, Cerberus, himself, pursued me.

Light flashed before me; my skin tingled like nobody's business and had a headache to die for, but I was through the exit point; I was safe.

Without the voice that reached me even on such an isolated planet like the Destoian homeworld, I would have been toast; the speaker of that voice was my beacon and light.

He was the reason I was here. Allister was the 'why' to my everything.

"I had been there before," I said. "Twice."

"You've been there before?" a different voice asked in response. It triggered my headgear, and I found myself blinking into a bright light.

The clean filtered air, I longed for that too, and took in and inhaled a huge breath of the sanitized molecules that indicated I was no longer on that God-forsaken death trap of a planet.

My heartbeat regained its steady rhythm, and the alloy base chair restrained me while performing a full-body diagnostic on my person as it secured me in place.

A small breathing apparatus set above my head but, I wasn't injured and didn't require reassertion.

I was home.

I blinked, remembering that I had been asked a question.

"Yes," I said. "It happened to me twice – the same words, the same drink, the only difference was Allister had on a blue shirt, not a brown one," I recalled my botched mission.

"Did you get the information?" The Master prompter in charge of my debriefing asked.

I nodded my head. "I'm not certain that it's as important as you say, Sir. Something seemed to be mixing up the signals – I couldn't tell the first time. I think that's why I was sent me back in," I said as I attempted to reason it out myself.

I glanced over the beam meant to disorient me as I studied the men behind the glass wall.

The Master Prompter's voice I hadn't recognized.

It wasn't the Commander's, though – I would know if he had been in the room just by the sound of his heartbeat.

I shifted as the alloy metal hands discontinued their probes and released me. The sounds dissipated, and I was able to lock onto the voice that had always been my saving grace.

"The Commander's not here?" I asked. He was lucky he wasn't – he owed me one after that stunt.

"No, he was held pressing matters elsewhere," the voice said.

'I bet,' the voice inside my mind interjected.

"You gave enough to save the insurgents from killing a whole planet – we owe you, Lieutenant," the Master Prompter concluded his interrogation.

'The hell you do – don't forget it,' the voice said that listened in as he added his two cents to the conversation.

I sighed.

"You're free to go," the Master Prompter said as he ended our debrief session.

Lights faded, and the buzzing overhead becomes almost non-existent. A familiar tingling sensation drifted throughout my core;

I had experienced it a hundred times before while I focused on the connection that had always been my lifeline.

My world faded to black; lights seeped under my closed eyelids, and I relaxed and reopened my eyes.

We were situated near the back of the restaurant, the ambiance filtered about me. Dimmed amber lights and a string quartet played an intergalactic classic.

I was back at the table with Allister. I felt slightly nauseous and disgusted at what I had learned. My head snapped up – his eyes devoured me.

My heart leaped to my throat before I took my finger off the trigger of my Glock. I was safe. I accepted the fact that my

Commander believed he had used me to interact with that thing.

I got it all. But, it also meant that my government had plans to replace my partner. I couldn't forgive that. A pretty dirty move, if I had to say so myself.

They had tried to use me to get to Allister. It made me a little heated under the collar too.

"Umm, hmm." Someone cleared their throat.

I glanced up and sought his eyes once more. It was a different restaurant.

This time it was a woman that stood over me waiting to take my order.

"Champagne?" Allister suggested.

My boyfriend's eyes twinkled. And, I had felt like celebrating.

"Did for you give me hell?" he asked.

"You've deserved worse," I said, hinting at our shared missions.

"I can't believe they thought I wouldn't notice if you weren't there." I retorted.

I could sense Allister has something he wanted to share – we shared chemistry.

"Let's leave this place," Allister said and stood as his strong hand reached to pull me after him.

"Never mind the drinks," he said, and turned, and winked at the waitress.

A slow blush crept to her ears and around her cheekbones, while her eyes conveyed the disappointment of not being able to attend the hero of Elasha.

I wasn't immune either, and I just had a lot of confidence and ability to connect to his thoughts – focused on me.

I felt a little giddy too. I had even felt bad for the waitress who couldn't stare into eyes so gray they appeared silver. See, I wasn't the jealous type unless I needed to be.

Because half the time, I contradicted myself and my feelings when it came to Allister's ability to put on the charm.

My boyfriend, after all, was the first Cyborgenic living specimen in the entire network that makes up the Galactic system, Nuevo.

His attraction was universal, and many desired his arsenal of services as well as his company.

Still, I was the one he loved. I had been the one that achieved the chemical makeup to trigger his neuro responses.

Allister was alive because he sought me. But it was a two-way street; I was alive because he found me, trained me; made me a part of him.

The galaxy's governments may have wanted to seek us both because we were the only two that could communicate through distances.

We were the sole beneficiary of a specific skill set and deadlier than twenty agents of the realms.

Yet, we shared something that no couple could ever share, and I would have died a long time ago without his unprecedented integration.

He called it a 'Life-merge.' I called it 'my blessing.'

"The next time you duplicate yourself for a mission, try and not leave out crucial details," I reprimand my lover.

"You noticed the shirt?" Allister asked as he laughed at me.

"Not right away – I noticed that your eyes were black," I added.

"Damn!"

"It's okay. It wasn't your fault. The Commander thought he could send your real duplicate elsewhere and replace that one with a copy they're testing. The next time they send me back, you come with me. Don't let them send in a replacement – I almost didn't make it," I said.

"That's going too far, Steele – are you okay?" Allister asked as he reached for me.

His concern etched into his features, and it made me feel guilty. I didn't need him to worry about me too.

"As 'right' as rain,'" I replied a little too cheerful.

"Good – let's go see how wet you are after going through

the Storm!" There was a glint in Allister's eyes.

"But, there will be no next time," Allister whispered as his lips touched mine.

It was a rare occasion when he allowed me full access to his thoughts.

Yeah, I know that I shared more with him than anyone else, but even Cyborgs had issues with opening up; showing human 'feelings.'

A tear escaped, but I quickly wiped it away. We had both made it out. The thing was – I realized what Allister was telling me.

"I'm not sending you in again, and we're not going back," he said.

I felt like celebrating. "Let's take the Champagne with us," I said and turned to the waitress who stood in the background who was 'fan-Girling.' My lover kissed me once more, and together we shifted. There was no way in hell I could go back, and besides, the Commander owed us. Allister had taken care of it. And in a way, so had I.

I didn't drink the water. Allister would never have reached me in time if I did. Freedom felt remarkable. I hadn't realized how shackled Allister and I actually were because I had always thought we were making a difference.

I would tell him about the 'water' incident when we were too far away for him to burn down the galaxy we were so desperately attempting to save. I knew we would have to seek someplace in the universe – someplace in time where those in command would never expect us to be.

It was a moot point to worry about it now. The galaxy would have to find itself another hero.

THE END

THE ONE

I used to berate myself all the time that the reason I couldn't remember anything or anyone before my sixteenth birthday was that I was sort of dumb. I could explain the dumb in me as just a typical teenager, but my memory loss.

That had me stumped. Only, I wasn't dumb or forgetful, and I was just ignorant of the fact that demons, magic that made one forget, along with alternative worlds, existed.

Big difference. In hindsight, I'd go back to ignorant, dumb, and forgetful; any of those things if it meant I could take back the choices that led to my inability to face myself in the mirror.

It's like realizing if you open a door and find out it's raining outside, you must choose; do you venture out and get wet, or do you stay inside, safe, and warm?

I'd go further. What if you couldn't stay inside, like what was outside meant your survival? What if even though you stayed inside and kept warm and dry, you died because you didn't have any food or water, and the water had been right out the door.

Damn, life gave some messed up scenarios. I guess it then depended on how brave a person chose to become. The choices were always there, and if the wrong decision were made, it could kill you.

People should always plan for the unexpected, but I'm not the one to preach to the choir; I had my choices stolen, and I suffered from the consequences.

My aunt certainly had a plan in mind when it came to raising me. So, she trained me like I was to become her one-woman commando unit.

I wondered about her allowing me that sort of training a lot back then. What had she been hiding from? My imagination sought different explanations; was she a spy for the CIA? And, other times, I believed her to be part of a vigilante group. I mean, the weapons she carried weren't something a 'normal' person could just get a hold of.

Yet, I was never brave enough to put her on blast or ask why I needed to run a five-mile stretch of beach in less than twelve minutes. I followed orders and became good at what I could and prayed it was good enough.

Had I known what I was training for, I would have run for the hills or the closest insane asylum.

'Stay ready, so you won't have to get ready,' my aunt would remind me whenever I slacked off, which made me too afraid to ask the question, 'ready for what?'

'You're special, Sage. You will have to face that someday,' she drilled these words into me too.

The funny thing was that I realized what my 'special' was only after being kidnapped and nearly killed. Then I got a whole bucket load of 'crazy' handed to me, so much so that my brain couldn't handle it.

And, Kablam! Total recall. I was a princess, and my aunt was a sorceress from another realm. And I was supposed to have been betrothed to a prince named Sealtiel, who I remembered I had loved with all my heart and soul even though we fought like cats and dogs.

That part of my story seemed sort of cool until it turned out I was prophesied over and found out why someone was attempting to kill me was because a demon wanted to hook up with me to take over the world by creating a bunch of baby demons that could create portals with their blood just like me – gross.

This caused a stir in Demon land, and my realm and all kinds of minions of evil wanted to end my existence before I mated their boss permanently. Because that meant there would be no stopping his takeover, and everyone knew demons didn't like to be told what to do.

And, I had to come to terms with a few facts of my own; my race – I wasn't human. My memory loss resulted from my family's attempt' to hide my whereabouts by sending me to the Outer Farther Reaches.

I was supposed to have some sort of connection with the unnatural creatures that existed in my world, which is why they sought the magic in my blood, magic that could reach through universes.

My people lived in the Inner Farther Reaches on the Isles of Crisette because demons lived on the mainland. We had survived because the Aquilian Ocean existed as a barrier that kept our enemies from reaching our homes.

We called them the Sha Drugons, and they were intricately connected to Shade, a version of Demon in the Outer Farther Reaches. As for the Sha Drugons, they abhorred water.

Our kind remained safe from these soul stealers that thrived on the mainland of theTau Nau's Brakes because of this one irrefutable fact.

I had been given the time necessary to hone my talents against Shade by the High Keepers, who were the only beings capable of using magic in our world.

My aunt, Val Ternie, was the last female sorcerer, and her job had been to train me when my magic awakened.

Still, my aunt could protect me no longer. And, I certainly wasn't safe in the Outer Farther Reaches, either.

Neither could I pretend that I hadn't caused Shade to empower the Sha Drugons to cross the Aquilian Ocean, something they hadn't been able to achieve in over a hundred years of their existence.

It was like waking up out of your worst nightmare when there was a certainty that nothing would ever compare to it. Until one's eyes opened and found reality had been much worse. Where the immersion of one's reality and the dream became one's living hell, remembering my past was like that. It brought heartache and suffering.

But it wasn't as if I could avoid the trigger because I was also irrevocably tied to an entity known as Shadow.

And, if it took the rest of eternity to open that damn gate again, Shadow owed me, and Sealtiel, big time.

The magic I awakened wasn't just any magic, but Blood Magic; I opened portals by way of my blood.

Only Shadow had left out the details – my power to keep a portal open had its time limits. And, using my blood to open the gates of Kesnel e Torin worked only twice.

A one-way ticket in and a one-way ticket out that held a catch. Once my magic dissolved, I could only reestablish the portal by taking the life's blood of another – a total blood sacrifice.

That sad ending was what had led me to this moment.

Blood pooled into my fisted palm from the point of my self-inflicted wound as I gathered enough of the precious liquid to make a rune around me and the entity that followed me like a faithful dog everywhere I went.

He was Shadow as well as my Shadow-Sworn, and yet I no longer trusted him, which proved problematic since we had made an irrevocable pact, tied to the other for eternity.

I had become something other than a Princess of Bi'Naleen, which had always been a title that I strove to ignore and prove that I was also capable of becoming, the Sword-Sworn of the Left Hand to the King of Neva Ehwen; the Sword-Sworn of the Right Hand was Sealtiel, my betrothed.

We had entered the Pact with Shadow together, hoping that gaining magic meant that we could protect our people from the rabid demon hordes of the Sha'Drugon ruled by Shade.

Sealtiel and I had believed in a lot of things back then; none of it had helped when it came to facing a betrayal we could never see coming. No matter how many lifetimes we had to prepare.

And while I was no longer worried about mortality, it wasn't a luxury to live forever. Instead, I labeled my ability and life a curse.

The High Keepers prophesied both Sealtiel and me to hunt down Shade, an enemy that only grew stronger because I had helped unleased the strongest Shade of all not only into my realm, the Inner Farther Reaches, but beyond, into the Outer Farther Reaches as well.

While in the Deeper Inner Reaches where Kesnel e'Torin lay, I had committed a horrendous act; my blood had allowed the King of Shade and his minions to escape.

And in the ensuing battle that followed, Sealtiel had been left behind because of the one law upon the 'gate' that allowed any to enter, had also been the law that demanded that someone must be sacrificed for any to leave.

Shadow had determined who that 'one would be. It left my betrothed behind in that lonely place to suffer for my stupidity and naivety – something I would never become again.

Sealtiel was only trapped in that horrible place due to the laws of the gate that held an equivocal exchange for any soul that entered the gate or exited, but my magic was strong.

I could create another condition inside the gate if I found the one soul that gate would accept as an exchange for Sealtiel's soul – easy.

And while it meant I had an eternity to locate what I searched for to set things right, my incredible talent held me to restrictions that bond me like a vice.

I had sworn that I would set right the bitter betrayal that separated my betrothed and me from one another. I would hunt down and return the King, and his minions to Kesnel e' Torin, the realm of the dead.

And I was prepared for the fallout. With my last breath if I had to, or with the last drop of blood in my veins if it came down to it.

Trusting Shadow had backfired. And, until I could track down the entity Shade that escaped during a botched rescue, Sealtiel would remain as the equivocal exchange for opening a portal meant to remain closed.

Despite my inner conflict, If I couldn't hunt down Shade and its vicious leader, then the Inner and Outer Farther Reaches were done for.

I wasn't the naïve' princess any longer, sacrifices were called for, and I had set my resolve in stone. I vowed to hunt down Shade and every demonic soul connected to its evil until I satisfied the laws of Kesnal e' Torin's gate.

There was no place for Shade or its underlings to hide, and even onto the Outer Farther Reaches, I would continue until I found them all.

And at this moment, the Shade King's demonic soul was the one soul I sought.

Pushing my Blood magic to the limits, Shadow and I entered the portal. The planet's dust was the color of burnt sienna; it blew in swirls like waterspouts, and breathing was nearly impossible on the surface of Tantora.

The smell of blood entered my nostrils; some dripped onto my clothing; I looked back at the blood-infused portal and shivered.

I pulled a breathing apparatus from my pouch and placed it over my face. My magic had brought me here; this planet had to be the Demon's hiding place – it had to be the one.

Either way, we had fifteen minutes; things would turn ugly after that. I looked back at the void of darkness that indicated my portal was invisible to any passerby – I didn't have much time.

Shadow accompanied me but stayed at a discreet distance; even so, it remained cloaked. It was for the best.

No sane individual would come to this awful place unless it were a death wish. I couldn't entertain that reason.

A guide met us proficient in 'earth-speak,' a dialect amongst those who traveled intergalactic and needed the means to communicate.

The creature was sure of his surroundings, and it placed me at ease as I followed alongside him as he led us through the dark lit streets of the derelict planet's housing district before leaving us at a small shanty near a back alley just on the outskirts, where sentries paid little attention to the coming or going of strangers.

I removed my breathing apparatus and wished that I hadn't; unpleasant odors, both foul, and rotten bombarded my sensitive nostrils.

My feet stalled at the single-entry doorway – no one was waiting for us.

The room where Shadow and I were to wait was insignificant in a general sense if it weren't for the dark mahogany wood desk that struck me as beautiful, immaculate – old, but so out of place on a planet such as Tantora that it stood out like the proverbial light that attracted a moth to a flame.

I whirled on our guide, "Where is he?" my voice a hoarse whisper.

I had twelve minutes left.

"So...so...sorry, Princess – be a moment. Nothing more. He is quick?" the guide repeated, fearful that I might renege on his payment.

"He had better be here – quick," I retorted at the poor creature that cowered but recovered enough to accept the payment I tossed him.

He flew out of my sight, shutting the door quietly behind him even in his haste.

Shadow sought the darkest part of the room, and I stifled any outburst at the impatience that sliced through me because our contact was late.

The chair creaked as if in protest when I sat, even though I was one hundred and twenty pounds soaking wet.

I swiveled about, and faced the lone window in the room, and looked out while the Dragasi moon crossed in front of Dresani, its twin.

An ominous sign? Death's sending?

Shadow shifted; it wanted my attention. I ignored it.

I had nothing left but hope and clung to it by a thread. I didn't need Shadow's reminder; time was running out.

Shade was transforming as it connected to other life forms; not only was it able to integrate its evil and coexist with its host, but once Shade latched on to an individual's soul, the only way to end their suffering was by death.

The Demon King Controlled Shade to reincarnate itself as many times as necessary into a living soul. He was hard to track down like a needle in a haystack because of it.

He could be anywhere in the Outer Farther Reaches, but I couldn't stop searching – ever.

I wouldn't say it caused me sleepless nights, but I hated it. Ending another's life because of its contact with Shade. A part of me died with each soul that I had to end; I was the reason Shade had infected them in the first place.

But, there wasn't an alternative recourse when dealing with a soul tainted by Shade. The person's soul was already lost, and removing Shade before it ascended to corrupt another soul was the only wrong I could undo.

Killing twisted me into tight little knots, and I never saw me reaching this destination – what sane person could? But weren't those souls technically already dead?

I had to believe that what I had been forced to become, what Shadow and I were forced to do, was the right thing – I had to.

At some point, I had shaken off the guilt.

I had become something other with no moral compass when it came to Shade's destruction. I would save Sealtiel no matter what it cost my soul.

It was either Shade or me, and even though I worked diligently to fortify my magic, would it be enough to capture the ruler of Shade long enough to return him unharmed and satisfy the laws of the Kesnel e' Torin's gate?

Still, I realized it wasn't my resolve at stake at all; it was Sealtiel's freedom.

I looked at my watch – ten minutes.

Anxiety churned in my stomach; my contact was late – where was he?

Time wasn't my enemy, but it dodged my footsteps like one.

A knock at the door made me swivel about. "Enter!" I stood.

My contact had arrived. His large frame swallowed the entryway before he stiffened and walked into the room.

A thin dark vapor-like mist fluttered over his silhouette before seeping into his nose and mouth; the smell of Shade was sickening.

I wondered had Shadow caught the scent; it was so subtle that it was barely noticeable in the already stale, moon-lit room.

The creature's eyes considered me, and my first reaction was strictly instinct – survival. I held back the bile that rose in my throat.

'*Was he who I had been searching for?*' Something screamed inside of me that he had to be the one.

"Are you the one?" I asked. I had to know. I also wondered would he acknowledge my skill to track him to this piece of a desolate, crappy planet. Was he surprised that I had tracked his scent down through the galaxies, using every ounce of magic I possessed to do so? Would he lie to me?

The carrier of Shade grew even more arrogant in his regard of me.

'*Try me!*' I wanted to yell. Instead, I asked once more. "Are. You. The. One?"

I was down to eight minutes.

"Things have changed, Princess Sage," the creature said.

He knew me; he knew who I was – I grew hopeful.

"How so, Dopin Mongar?" I asked. I knew him as well. Or who he used to be before Shade channeled into his soul.

The creature toppled over the chair, rising with alarm as recognition at what I was about filtered into its empty soul while I worked away to undo the magic that would uncover its subterfuge.

Hatred filtered into its eyes. "You brought this on yourself, but you no longer have to search for what you seek. I only carry a message from our King," he said and smiled.

"He's not my 'King,' I spat. He had me –he wasn't the one.

My heart dropped at what his words meant.

"I will tell you where to find your Shade King. He waits for you on Asheron," the Dopin Mongar said.

"Then you've wasted my time," I said and stood and walked past the carrier of Shade toward the door.

Six precious minutes remained.

There was no sound; there never was, but I turned about all the same. The Dopin Mongar lay dead in his seat. His eyes registered surprise – he hadn't seen Shadow's reckoning.

I nodded. "Bring the body. It carries Shade," I spoke to Shadow. No way was I placing my thoughts into its mind in a shared telepathic link; I no longer trusted anything it had to share with me.

Shadow's black wings rose in agitation at my audacity to command it to do anything, but I was too devasted to care. Besides, my Blood Magic was losing its potency.

We would have to chance the sentries after all, and on the run at that, we had two minutes remaining.

The Demon King hadn't used the Dopin Mongar to insert its twisted soul into its body but used its essence to lead me on another wild goose chase.

A tear escaped to wet my cheek; I felt so weary.

My eyes shot to the door, and I wheeled out into the dusty corridor of a forsaken planet on a dead run. No matter how long it took, I'd find the Shade King and rescue Sealtiel.

Thirty seconds.

Slipping through the portal as it slammed shut, my breath jammed back down my throat, and my limbs felt like putty as they wobbled underneath me.

I truly felt no remorse, as long as I could make it through the next portal and the next.

Shadow held back its retort, barely. I grimaced before I dropped to my knees, glancing upward as the fading blood-red veil that made up the rune spewed out the last drops of my blood.

It splattered just inches from my fingers. I was fatigued to the point of exhaustion, weak as a kitten, my heartbeat with an irregular rhythm, and my hands were cold.

I knew the signs that meant I had drained the blood inside my body dry as I pushed myself to the limits. And, I would need another transfusion soon as I felt my magic unraveling –withering from overuse.

The Dopin Mongar was just another pawn used by Shade, but he had given me the first hint to ending my perpetual nightmare.

He had been right about one thing, though; he was not the one.

THE END

THE FALL

I was told to expect a surprise. I didn't care for surprises – my brother knew this. The type of surprises I received almost always ended up being just the opposite – bad shockers.

Still, I showed up. I was only here because Ander needed my help. His guilt about selling my aunt's home had been a no-brainer because she had allowed us to stay with her when my mom died, and my father had a breakdown because of it.

We owed Aunt Ossie a lot, but it ended there. I knew he wanted to salvage the place or maybe give it to my uncle, but I'd rather he'd just sell it and get it over with. I never wanted to step foot inside this house ever again.

I shouldn't have entered the house alone – bad memories lived here. And, waiting for my brother was a pain; he was always late. Still, it was too cold to remain in the car; it wasn't much better inside either.

The smell of rust, old paint, and mold hit me, which almost made me change my mind; the car was the better choice. Instead, I wrapped my arms around me and headed for the kitchen.

I took a quick look around; a recliner, couch, and other furniture were positioned around the living room; dust had settled on everything. The house would need a total renovation if Ander decided he wanted to keep it.

59

"At least Ander kept the power on," I said as if the sound of my voice would stop me from creeping out.

I turned, flipped a switch, and blinked into the gloom; the dim light chased away some shadows, but barely.

Cobwebs fluttered as I strode into the hall that led to the kitchen, walking around the dirtied area rug that showed signs it had seen its last days.

The house screamed of its 'neglect,' and I felt it was high time Ander took over and just sold it before there was no profit to be made.

"No way are we were keeping this house," I muttered; I almost missed the noise upstairs,

'Who left the TV on?'

"Jesus, Ander!" I swore under my breath; I knew my brother was irresponsible, but lately, I hadn't done much better in the accountability department.

I had also given up on expecting things to go smoothly when dealing with this house; I walked up the wooden stairs and headed toward the master bedroom.

Memories accosted me when I passed the door that used to be my bedroom, and I wasn't ready to face my past; I hoped I could bury that time in my life forever, but it wasn't healthy. It was also what shackled me to my pain.

I paused. Sure enough, I heard a commercial playing; the jingle I recognized as a Folder's commercial 'The best part of waking up,' I smiled. I could use a cup of coffee; maybe that was why I was so antsy; I had missed my daily brew.

I sighed and walked past my old bedroom. Ander had probably left it on when he stopped by yesterday. The place had been abandoned for the last three months – my uncle was nowhere to be found.

I took a few more hesitant steps and then another as I approached the master bedroom; I still couldn't shake the dread that had overcome me, especially when I came to the doorway.

"You're too old to be scared of ghosts," I scolded myself, but my steps faltered anyway.

"Stop being silly," I spoke a simple phrase of courage, and boldly entered the room, walked forward, and switched off the TV.

I was always 'hearing' things, but I hadn't imagined the shuffle behind me, though, and spun about – I wasn't alone.

'Shit!'

It was too late to defend myself as I caught the flash of something before it made contact with the side of my head.

"Oww!' I cried out.

The pain was intense too, and then mercifully, darkness came for me.

I came to with the TV blasting Bonanza's theme as someone leaned over my head, wheezing. My hands were tied behind my back with an extension cord and tied so tight that I felt my fingers tingling; there was no way I could pull myself free, and I tried.

The chair I was propped in had been one of my aunt's favorite; it was still old, and I had forgotten how rickety the arms were; the seat padding was barely there.

My stomach churned, and my anxiety was out of control. I had been in a sorry place in my head for so long that I was in denial that I could ever become a decent human being. Even God knew that I hated myself more than I could ever love myself.

I glanced up at the man that had caused so much of my pain and insecurities, wondering how I could ever make up for what was done to me when I was twelve years old.

"Cash? Whatcha doing here?" my uncle asked. I almost retched from the stench of him; he smelled of vodka and beer, and his clothes were rancid and reeked of sweat and urine.

"Uncle Jess?" I shifted my head sideways to get a better look at him, but the effort it took hurt so bad that I closed my eyes. My uncle looked terrible – much worse than I remembered.

He bent over me, checked my head to see if he had seriously injured me. He took his sweet time rubbing his meaty hands near the base of my neck, and I shifted to the side.

"Don't touch me!" I hissed.

"It alright, Baby Girl," Uncle Jess whispered as he called me by a name I had hoped never to be vocalized from his lips ever again.

I shuddered as he continued to rub his hands down my arm. "Why you come back?" he asked, his voice slurred from alcohol as he wiped at the blood caused by a gash near my temple.

"It's bleeding, Cash – shouldn't have hit you so hard," he slurred again.

I clenched my teeth and focused on my breathing; I could tell my injury was bad, but it wouldn't end me.

In a way, I wish he had – killed me.

Because I knew with certainty that I would end his miserable life the next time he touched me. I yanked my head away from his hands and moaned. "Uncle Jess...why are you here?" I asked as I fought against the binding around my wrist and attempted to stand.

"Whoa, Pretty Girl, you took quite a hit to the head; you can't be standing yet. I didn't hurt you any. You young enough to get over that," he muttered.

Uncle Jess was between borderline wasted and stone-cold drunk. Even though all I wanted to do was get away from him, my mind wasn't working, and my head was killing me.

I attempted to hold my breath when he moved too close; the rancid smells only got worse. What had he been doing all this time?

Gagging, I sucked in my breath as Uncle Jess knelt over me and commenced to remind me how much I enjoyed when I was a little girl and how I loved when he rubbed between my legs.

"Uncle Jess? I think I'm going to be sick," I whispered. There was no telling what I would do if I continued talking; I wanted to yell and scream that I was 'fucking twelve years old,' what could I have loved about any of that?

I shook my head; my eyes watered, and bile triggered a reflex reaction. I tried to hold it back.

My uncle was drunk and rambling gibberish, and I wanted to do was place my hands around his neck and let him see how messed up he had made me; how I couldn't even love myself like I should have because of what he had done to the twelve-year-old me. I sobbed. "Uncle Jess? You hear me. I need to throw up?"

"No, you don't. You always making excuses to get away from me – you can't leave me no more," he whined.

I needed to calm down, or I wouldn't be able to talk my way out of this mess. And no one was going to save me; I had to protect myself like always.

"Uncle Jess, why are you here...what happened to the money Ander sent you?" I asked. My voice broke; I attempted to sound all grown up and unafraid – I was twenty-five, for Christ's sake.

I was almost certain Uncle Jess was in the mindset to subject me to something unimaginable. Something I had fought most of my adult life to heal over.

I stood up; the extension cord bit into my wrist, but I attempted to make a run for it anyway.

Uncle Jess pushed me back into the chair. "Be still a girl! You gonna make me hurt you again. Why you have to come back and take what should be mine, Colene don't need you or that brother of yours taking nothing from me. She died! This house be mine!" Uncle Jess yelled as his eyes fixated on me.

The hair on the back of my neck stood on end as he reached down to touch my face.

"Like you mine now, you come back because you miss me?" Uncle Jess slurred the last part of his rant, waving an empty beer bottle in the air.

I kicked out, sending my uncle flailing back. '*The Bastard hit me with a beer bottle.*'

"Dammit, Girl, stop fighting me!" Uncle Jess said as he came at me; I ducked my head and closed my eyes.

"Uncle Jess, you've been drinking," I cried, waiting for him to hit me, but he never did.

I didn't care that I made him upset because something inside me snapped. I wasn't the twelve-year-old girl that never said a word anymore.

Uncle Jess reached for my breast. "Don't touch me!" I yelled. "Uncle Jess, you can't do this anymore. Just let me go, please. I won't tell Ander," I pleaded

Uncle Jess shook his head. "You not telling nobody nutting, you here!"

I nodded. "I'm not, I promise. I won't tell Ander, and I'll talk him into letting you keep the house, okay?" I asked.

Uncle Jess laughed. "Girl, I don't care bout stuff like that. You here with me now. You know I got to get back up inside you once more; all I could think about is my sweet Cassandra, you miss me, girl, hmm? Uncle Jess asked.

Then he bent and kissed me on the mouth. There was no way I could keep back the bile.

I spewed chunks into his face as he recoiled back, wiping at my vomit with a look of complete surprise before his eyes turned murderous.

"Ungrateful Bitch," Uncle Jess said as he reared his arm back and punched me in the face.

I crashed to the floor as the old chair broke apart – wooden slates flew everywhere.

I hadn't yelled out, but I hurt all over, and then I started to gag on my vomit. *"I was going to die!'*

God, I hoped I could kill my uncle before I gave up the ghost. My eyes teared, but I refused to admit defeat; instead, I started to laugh.

Uncle Jess was drunk enough to laugh with me as he untied the extension cord and helped me to sit on the floor.

Horrible memories flooded through me from what my uncle had done to me, and I started to sob.

"Cash, you be quiet now. I ain't about to hit you no more; I just need you to clean yourself up," Uncle Jess said as he tried to help me up, but I whirled on my back and kicked him in the balls.

He yelled something at me and grabbed hold of the beer bottle, but I ducked out from under his reach, leaped to my feet, and ran for the door.

I was too scared to look behind me as my feet carried me down the hall; my legs felt like jelly, and I was lightheaded and disoriented even as blood dripped into my eye from the cut on the side of my head.

I crashed into the railing at the top of the stairs as Uncle Jess caught me and grabbed my collar from behind.

"Come here!" he grunted and yanked me down; I fell backward as my head bent over the top of the stairs; I fought back, but Uncle Jess was too big, too strong – too drunk.

My scream died in my throat as Uncle Jess pulled me against the railing and pinned me down; his fist crashed into my face as he repeatedly punched me.

Blood squirted everywhere, and Uncle Jess's featured blurred; his face distorted.

"Stop! I'm not going to let you!" I shoved my hands in front of me; I wasn't going to be dragged back to the bedroom. No way!

Uncle Jess finally let up; when I yelled at him, he stared at me as if he had just realized that he was close to beating me to death.

"Cash? Why you make me go and do that?" he asked.

His heavy pants mixed in with my sobs were the only sound in the empty house.

"Why you get sick?" Uncle Jess asked. He rubbed the cloth over my face and chest to remove the vomit while I continue to dry heave.

That was when he tore another piece of cloth and shoved it into my mouth. Tears streamed down my face, and I was certain my eye was permanently damaged.

Uncle Jess stood and wrapped his hand around my bra in an attempt to drag me back down the hall – back toward the bedroom.

All I felt was pathetic, just like the twelve-year-old girl back then, desperate to have God send me a Guardian Angel. I learned early on not to believe in stuff like that; I was as pathetic now as I was back then.

"I don't need anybody to save me!" I sobbed as I fought for my life, pushing my uncle off me with a strength born out of desperation, and reached for the railing.

I caught the crook of my elbow between the wooden rail and dug in as my uncle tugged.

"Let go!" he yelled.

I shook my head no, as blood, snot, and tears marked my face.

That banister was the only thing keeping me alive, and I wasn't letting go. The crazy inside my head also began to play out scenarios that left no room for the imagination.

I was better off dead. *'No. Please, Uncle Jess – No'*

And then I heard the door open downstairs, and my brother's eyes met mine.

"Let her go!" Ander yelled as he took the steps two at a time.

The banister groaned and creaked against the strain of my body, and with the extra weight that Uncle Jess's placed on the old banister, it wasn't going to hold both of us.

Distracted by Ander, I grabbed my uncle; he wasn't going to hurt my brother as he hurt me. When the railing gave way, my uncle looked at me with his eye bulging out of his head because I pulled him with me as the banister gave way.

My brother reached for me, and I smiled at him; it would be okay, I wanted to tell him.

A sense of righting a wrong washed over me; finally, I fought back to avenge when my twelve-year-old self couldn't. Falling felt sort of gratifying; I was finally free. Still, even that freedom was short-lived.

The impact as my back hit the recliner before I crashed onto the wooden floor, snapping my head back; it left my body a broken mess.

White-hot heat seared through my head and neck, and my spine felt like it was on fire. My vision blurred as colorful spots 'or were they stars?' danced in front of my eyes.

I had heard my uncle's blood-curdling scream echoed somewhere beside me as his drunken body landed brokenly next to my own – it was over.

I rolled my head to the left and tried to open my swollen eyes so that I could get a good look at my uncle's body. His face was twisted in agony, and his eyes stared upward as if he too were surprised that I had taken him with me over the railing.

I sniffed and reached forward, stretching my fingers toward my uncle even as the pain shot up my arm, which caused me to almost blackout.

My eyes fixated on Uncle Jess's unblinking eyes; he wouldn't be hurting anyone anymore.

"Sis!" I heard Ander call my name as he staggered down the wooden steps to reach me.

"Ander?" I breathed his name; I wanted to tell him that I was sorry. Everything appeared so dim, but not quite dark; it was just full of shadows. It wasn't so bad.

An angelic male voice called my name as he stepped out of the darkness, as he urged me to follow him, but I shook my head no. Not yet.

I couldn't go with him even though I had recognized him; I knew him. 'My Angel.'

His smile conveyed a sadness that mimicked mine; it was okay, I was going to be okay. My Guardian Angel watched me waited for me.

'I'm sorry,' I sighed.

'Everything is okay now,' he replied as the wind brushed cool against my fevered body.

Movement in the distance caught my attention as I made out a door filled with light, brightening my path.

'Wow, it's so beautiful,' I whispered. I had envisioned a lighthouse's light – the light I saw mirrored its ability to bring hope when there was only darkness before.

There was no more guilt or shame and no more storms to fear – I was safe.

My brother's sobs reached me, but I couldn't comfort Ander, but I wished he could see what I saw.

'It's okay. God is waiting on me.'

"Hold on, Sis," my brother said. I felt his love flooding past the darkness as the Guardian Angel let go of my hand.

'It seems it's not time to go yet,' My Guardian Angel explained.

'Okay,' I whispered.

I found it a miracle that the twelve-year-old girl faced me and smiled as she turned and took my Guardian Angel's hand.

It was time for her to depart, and she waved goodbye and blew a kiss my way.

'Goodbye,' I called after her as I watched. Pain, shame, guilt, and regret went through that door with her – it was over.

Dark shadows flitted across my vision; angry gust and scary billowing wisps burst forth to entangle my uncle's body.

Demon ghosts appeared like willow wisps and smoke tendrils that formed shapes of grotesque creatures with gaping maws.

They picked up my uncle's body plucking from him his soul; his flesh and eyes were sunken as if his soul had been pulled from his body.

Another presence hovered near the demons; Darkness materialized into a dark skin goliath, a seven-foot monster with a scythe and an obsidian sword.

Eyes like molten lava glanced in my direction, my soul burned hot, but I averted my gaze, closing my eyes tight.

Then I heard a door open, and I reopened my eyes, only to find that Uncle Jess was gone.

In the distance, a billowing dark cape carrying a dead body entered a gateway. Death turned back one last time to gaze at me; I felt blessed that he overlooked my sins, that he decided to allow me to live.

The doorway slammed shut – there was no light on the other side.

THE END

THE DRAGON SHIFTER

CHAPTER ONE – ARNARI

THE SIEGE

Blood splatters hit me in the face, and I tried not to flinch, but at the vulnerable age of fifteen, I could only pretend to be so brave.

It wasn't the first experience I wanted to remember during my first battle, either. I did what I could to wipe the spattering aftertaste of salt and rust off my lips.

My eyes scan my surroundings; it's so hectic that I don't even have time to be frightened, although I know it wasn't normal what I was witnessing by any means.

The amount of blood spilled in such a short manner of time on either side had been mind-blowing. The roar of the battle had quieted down some as we entered the abandoned gates of Doret.

This was the Kingdom my father wished to destroy along with the whole of its people. There had been no talks of peace or surrender as far as I could tell, and because it was my first battle, I am to get in as much 'training' as possible while there was still blood to be had. I knew nothing about war; only people died, and the conquerors gained more power, but witnessing such brutality offered just the right amount of reality to sober a drunk.

As a warrior race, our people prided themselves on producing both men and women fit for battle. Still, because of my station, next to my brother, I was expected to exceed the simple title of warrior – magic stirred in our veins.

My eyes scan my surroundings taking in the screams of the dying along with it. It was nothing like what my father and brother could prepare me for without the firsthand account that comes with experience; I will have to make a kill today.

At first, I was only supposed to observe and never leave my brother's side, but things have a way of not going according to plan, especially if you on a horse and dragons are diving in for the kill splattering blood me.

"Keep your eyes on the sky," my brother warned.

"I'm trying," I said as my attempt to hold the oversized silver roan under tight rein seemed almost laughable. Thank goodness, he was better trained than me.

I squinted at the sky, nervous, uncomfortably warm, and profoundly aware that my life remained in question. My horse and I were covered in blood and surrounded by fire.

The horse and rider to my right had ended up in the talons of an outraged dragon, and I felt lucky just to be alive.

"How much longer?" I asked because I didn't want to be the first to cower in fear, even if this was the first war I had ever been a part of.

Technically I was more than willing just to be an observer, but fate seemed to have other plans.

"Until I say it's safe to ride," my brother steered his horse close to my own.

"Where's Father?" I asked.

Mal glared at me to be quiet. "He's dealing with their King. Just watch until this is over – be quiet for a change, Nari," my brother said.

I nodded my willingness to do as my brother said and wiped my face, managing to smear more blood across my face than remove it.

"Damn Shifters," a voice said to my left.

I turned my head toward Captain Jeril as he cursed our enemy; he stationed his stallion alongside Mal, and me motioning for us to dismount and follow.

"This is taking longer than we planned. I'm to lead you two to safety; stay put until I return," the Captain said. He nodded in the direction he wanted us to go, and I grabbed my bow and arrows and dismounted.

The air was choked with smoke and soot, and I covered my mouth with my hand as I followed behind my brother down a darkened alley.

"Captain? What type of wood is this that not even dragon's breath can char it?" I asked, curious how the heavy doors seemed untouched by the fires that ravaged everything else inside the city walls' interior.

"Our mages have contained the fires, don't worry, Princess. As long as you and the Prince stay put, you'll not be placed in harm's way," the Captain grunted his response.

I took it to heart that the last part of his reprimand was directed at me; I listened. Most times, at least.

The Captain took his shoulder to one of the back doors; it was sturdy in its making and barred us from entry for only a moment as it gave way with Mal's help.

My brother's magic combined with old-fashioned muscle as the Captain did the rest and forced his way inside.

"It's nice inside," I said as I looked around. It was somewhat surprising that this particular dwelling had large paintings and carpets made of the finest furs.

It appeared luxurious like our castle at home, even onto the silver dishware and silk curtains.

"Someone of importance lived here," I whispered.

"Imitators only who mimic high society. Remember Princess, these beings are vile creatures and should not be compared to our proper way of life," the Captain explained.

'Could have fooled me.' "Yes, Captain," I said.

It was hard to believe such simple-mindedness when the telltale signs were right before one's eyes. The layout of the home was impressive and was kept immaculately clean. Further, into the room, smooth white marble walls and shiny white stone tiles gleamed with care.

All three of us fit comfortably into what seems to be a foyer of some kind; it's at least as spacious as my room back home.

My brother reset the back door as blue light flickered at his fingertips; he was always good at Magic Wielding.

Unlike me, I had yet to show any signs of creating magic at all. I was still grateful that the bulk of solid wood blocked out the screams of those unlucky enough to find shelter.

"No one believed such abominations existed," Captain Jeril's eyes conveyed his hatred of the Dragon Shifters.

"Aren't they like us?" I asked as my brothers shot a glare my way.

"We use magic. These 'Creatures' change their bodies into abominations of evil. We Are Not the Same, Arnari," my brother said.

"I just mean, I know they don't use magic the same way but, it's magic all the same, isn't it?" I asked.

"Nari!" My brother shook my shoulders so hard, my teeth rattled. "Don't ever let Father hear you say that we're the same as the Shifters —he won't hesitate to make an example of you," he reminded me.

"I'm not afraid —"

"You should be, Nari. Don't say stuff like that!"

"Your brother is right, Princess." Captain Jeril's eyes raked down to me as if he believed me to be just as vile, and I shuddered.

"Your unfounded beliefs are foolish and will get you killed. Your Master Teacher may as well hand you your death sentence if he continues to teach you such nonsense," the Captain said.

"She's just trying to figure it all out," my brother said in defense of my outburst.

I was terribly ashamed and equally embarrassed that Mal had to defend my big mouth. "I'm sorry," I said. "I won't bring it up ever again – I promise."

"Let's just make it out of here alive; after today, it won't matter anyway. The last of the Shifters end with the death of their King," my brother said.

I shook my head, but it hadn't made me feel any better about the war that would annihilate the Dragonshifter's of Doret.

CHAPTER TWO – NARI

THE SHIFTER

Captain Jeril left Mal and me with a warning not to leave the building until he retrieved us. I found myself nodding, a little too eager to do exactly as he commanded.

When he left, my brother reeled about and glared at me, giving me a taste of a thousand words he never said aloud.

In return, I made a face at my brother and winked.

"Nari!"

"It's okay, Mal. I don't think Captain Jeril will tell Father. He's too worried about his station to get on your bad side," I said.

"One day that mouth of yours –"

"Yeah, yeah, I know," I laughed and spun about to find anything that would remove the blood off my face.

That's when I caught a glimpse of my appearance in a mirror.

"I look a mess," I said and cringed. "Is there any water around?" I asked.

I realized I was 'hopeful' that I could remove the spots from my hair and face, but a princess could try.

"Warriors don't care what they look like – only victory matters," my brother attempted to tutor me – as if I cared.

"Well, lucky for me that I'm a princess too," I stuck my tongue out to irritate my brother more.

"And, princesses are not crass," my brother reminded me.

"Yeah, yeah," I resorted to my fall back saying as I walked into a large kitchen.

"Looks like no one has been here for days," I made small talk but pulled up short as I noticed bread and cheese on the table half eaten and a chair overturned as if the person had to leave in a hurry.

"Looks like someone left in a hurry. I think it's fresh enough to eat – go clean up, I'll see if there's anything to go with that without making us sick," Mal said.

"They live as we do," I said.

My brother gave me an incredulous look to indicate that he thought I had lost my mind.

"I know. I know," I said. "I promised not to bring it up."

I knew I had just broken my promise not to bring up comparisons between the Shifters and us.

"Nari – go!"

"Mal –"

Mal held up his hand and motioned me to be quiet. "Shush. Did you hear that?" he asked.

He was already across the room and shoved aside a large rug that covered a hidden entry built into the marble floor.

The thump of my heartbeat grew noticeably louder because I certainly heard something too.

Mal pointed the tip of his sword as he caught the latch with its point and nodded that I stand to ready.

I wasn't exactly useless and notched my arrow and aimed as Mal squatted and pulled the latch free as the door sprung back and exposed what was hidden underneath the floor.

"Look out!" I yelled and took aim but didn't shoot as a pair of silver eyes stared into my own and stalled my hand.

Mal repositioned his blade and swung it up to deliver the fatal blow.

"Stop!" I yelled. "Mal – he's not armed."

"He's one of them!"

"He's just a boy and no older than me," I said, as my eyes pleaded with my brother.

The boy with the silver eyes hadn't reacted, and he didn't attempt to retaliate either.

His eyes followed me, though, before he glanced at Mal. His cheeks were tear stained.

My heart pounded in my chest, and even though I hadn't thought it through, I placed my bow down at my feet, and walked up to the edge of the trap door, and leaned over, offering my hand.

"Careful, Nari – you're too close," Mal hissed.

"I'm alright. He's not going to hurt me – are you?" I reached my hand out to the boy taking in his desperate stance. "I won't hurt you. You understand me, right?" I kept my hand extended, hoping he would take it and not maul me by biting it off.

Dragons did that, didn't they?

"Nari –

"It's okay, Mal; he's more afraid than anything." I looked back at the boy, unsure why I wanted him to know that he was safe, even if it was only for the time being.

"I bet that food was yours, wasn't it; are you hungry?" I asked.

I wasn't even sure what I was doing, only that I had a strong desire to protect the boy who looked at me with silver eyes.

The connection was so intense that I wondered did the silver-eyed dragon feel it too?

I also knew although I had stayed Mal's hand, it wouldn't be forever unless I could convince my brother that we should save him instead.

I didn't want to even think about if Captain Jeril returned before we could figure something out.

I looked at Mal, my eyes still pleading. "I know what Father thinks about this boy. That he and his kind are nothing but evil spawns, but he's not, Mal. I just know it," I pleaded.

I had Mal's attention, and at least he wouldn't strike the boy down, and so I turned my attention back to the boy.

"I'm Arnari," I said and kept my hand extended.

"That's my brother, Malan. We won't hurt you; are you okay?" I asked.

"You ask a lot of questions," the boy replied.

I swore at that moment that I had wanted to smack the smirk off his beautiful face but hesitated.

Wasn't I trying to save him? I coughed, distracted by the way his eyes locked onto mine and because of the melodic tone within his speech.

His voice sounded strange but, I understood him perfectly.

"You speak our language?" I glanced at Mal, who seemed just as surprised as me. "How?"

"My mother taught me," he said.

"Where is your mother now?" Mal tightened his grip on his sword and scanned the area.

"No one is here but me. I wanted to fight too, but my mother told me I wasn't ready. They've all left to fight the usurpers," the boy said.

"He means us," I whispered at my brother.

"Are you a Shifter?" I asked, unable to take my eyes off his beautiful face.

"My father is."

"And your mother?" Mal's eyes darted to mine as he shook his head for me to remain quiet.

"She came from a faraway place, Zatius, I think," the boy replied.

I blinked before my brother, and I both made eye contact.

"That's our sister Kingdom," my brother rose and paced the small area between where the boy stood in place inside the trap door.

"What do we do?" I asked my brother.

Mal stopped and stared at the boy for a moment before he narrowed his eyes.

"Hey, Shifter! Eyes off my sister," he said.

"Mal!" I huffed at his assertion that the boy was staring at me any other way than with curiosity.

"Father will kill him," Mal said, as he watched me before he went back to studying the boy who remained huddled in the hideaway.

"You might as well come up from there. It's not like we're going to hurt you now after all this time," Mal said and offered his hand.

The boy took it and climbed out of the cellar; his clothes fit him well, and he was taller than I had expected.

His attention had returned to Mal, and I felt a pang of longing that his eyes were no longer fixated on me.

Mal, in turn, held my gaze; I knew my brother well. But, something inside me wanted to spare the young boy; his eyes were a gorgeous color, and beyond even that? He just reached out to my heart in ways I couldn't even begin to understand.

"Hey? What's your name?" I asked, desperate to find a solution so that Mal wouldn't be used to eliminate him when our father learned of the half-shifter.

"What's yours?"

"My sister has told you already; you're insulting and ungrateful. Especially since I haven't buried my sword in your heart." Mal scoffed.

Mal seemed angry on my behalf, believing the boy could speak to me as he wanted, and I laughed.

"He reminds me of you," I said. "Proud even it earns him a sword through his heart – not caring it seems."

I beckoned to show him that it was okay for him to approach me. "I told you, I'm Arnari, and that's my brother Malan but, you can call me Nari."

The boy blinked once as his eyes darted to my hand, "You're covered in blood, you know," he said.

Mal's laughter made my ears grow hot, but I relaxed. Everything was going to be okay.

"It's okay, it's not mine," I said. I thought about it and realized that it was a little mean-spirited to mention something like that.

"We are enemies, so of course it wouldn't be yours," the boy returned.

I winced. "We. Were. Enemies. That is until you knew our names," I said, expecting him to hurry up and get used to it because – somehow we were going to save his Dragonhide.

"I'm S... – Zataray," he said, leaving out his unfinished name.

It didn't go unnoticed by either Mal or me but, I shrugged it off.

"Zataray, nice to meet you –" my words died in my mouth as the boy reached out, took my hand, and shook it.

I looked over at Mal. What was I supposed to do? No one touched a princess or prince without the offering of our hand first; it was new territory for me.

"Cat got your tongue, Nari?" my brother laughed, and it erased my unease.

The boy's hand covered mine. His clasp was warm, and I felt a tingling run up my arm before I snatched my hand back.

"Suck eggs!" I said.

"What now?" the boy asked. His grey eyes seemed so sad.

"Now we figure out how to get our father to save your Dragonhide," Mal said.

CHAPTER THREE – NARI

THE SHAMANS OF AVIDAN

I glanced back over my shoulder only to see the smoldering remains of what was once a thriving kingdom; its inhabitants all murdered. And my father led the slaughter.

No one was left alive; a whole of people were annihilated because they happened to use a different type of magic than our own. Has it become so easy to condone an entire race of people just because they were feared?

"Nari, pay attention," my father was speaking. "You and Mal will be solely responsible for that creature's upkeep – train him well."

"Yes, Father." When did I become so meek?

It was a miracle; I couldn't begin to count how many of those I've encountered since meeting Zataray. I look over at him, his horse following behind Mal. A servant of the Prince of Avidan; how is that lucky?

'Do you hate us? Now that we've killed your people. Do you forgive us because we spared your life? How can you be happy amongst your enemies?'

Zataray was right – we were enemies.

At least for now, I hoped he would allow me to make amends and somehow enable me to wipe the sadness from his soul somehow. If that was even possible?

"Nari!"

"I'm sorry, Father – I promise you that I am listening," I closed my eyes and blotted out the images of death.

"You did well for your first battle; continue your lessons and prove to me that you will hone your skills."

He hadn't mentioned that I hadn't honed a single skill set that suggested 'Magic Wielder,' a feat feared by all the remaining nine Kingdoms.

"Do you know why I don't speak up on your gift?" my father asked.

He had my attention, especially if he could read my mind so easily; I turned my eyes on him.

"The Shamans spoke of your birth – your magic will be like none other and will overshadow all that has come before. People will fear your power," my father said as he glanced back at the boy trailing after my brother. "That one was mentioned as well."

I started. "The Shamans spoke about Zataray?" I asked.

"A Half-blood who will never shift, but connected to your power somehow ¬ I dare not kill him until I know just what that connection is," my father grunted his reply as his eyes took on a menacing glare.

"Father, how can you tell he will never use shifter magic? Is that why he was spared?" I asked.

My father's eyes were cold as he spoke about Zataray's future. "As far as the Kingdom is concerned, Zataray was captured as a young boy and made to serve the Shifters – his identity dies with the evil that spawned him."

Growing up as a Princess, I was never spared from chastisement or earning any special treatment as I gained my place amongst the elite who fought for what Avidan stood for.

As I listened to my father's reasoning as to why Zataray was alive, I felt afraid. Fear seared through me for the fate of any who were different in any way that the King had not sanctioned.

And, I had believed my Father to be merciful – he was just ruthless and unforgiving. I had thought I understood what made a ruler; my Master Teacher attempted to forewarn me, but it took this act of cruelty for me to learn my first lesson about war.

My father's cruelty and decisive nature were what made him a king feared by all the nations. And his ability to make the tough calls and gain strength from his ability to judge and become a prosecutor.

Above all else, he would have a legacy that would seal his place in history. My father was the King who purged the evil from the land – killing all who defied him.

A mage peered into the future to save a Half-blood, and I want to be grateful but, it didn't make it right that a whole people died so that Zataray could live.

My father killed out of fear of the unknown; he destroyed a whole people's way of life because they were nothing like us but looked and lived just like us.

My father, the King, had ordered a massacre of women and children in cold blood to prove his stance over another's.

My Master Teacher always told me that War didn't show favoritism, nor did it recognize the color of one's soul.

Kind-hearted or not. War produced murderers even if the cause seemed justified at the time. The point was moot regardless.

Choices to kill or be killed, no matter the premeditation, always came at a high cost.

Solely acting according to a command to carry out an insidious act seemed a moot point, especially when the longing inside one's heart was based on survival.

Human nature wanted to survive at any cost, and the instinct to survive would always prevail.

The reality of the situation appeared simple; a people's bloodline has been wiped out, and there just wasn't any happy endings in Zataray's future.

I took part in this cowardly act out of conviction, and by choice, I sealed his fate.

And out of guilt, I offered my hand in friendship based upon a lie.

My heart cried for those souls that fought and died so that another's belief could be honored.

My father could justify such deaths as a befitting means to a necessary end.

I felt sorry for such narrow-minded individuals like my father.

But, then what I had done to save Zataray's life – I wasn't any better.

CHAPTER FOUR – ZATARAY

THE SECRET

Heat permeated my insides and expanded outward to flood me in pain. My body felt afire.

Voices condemn inside my mind condemned me a traitor, murderer, collaborator. They were not far off the mark.

I had lived and thrived in the camp of the enemy of my people, and guilt spread through me like a runaway blaze.

I was friends with my enemies.

And, I burned in the pit of despair as eyes full of accusations asked where lay the honor in how I lived and breathed.

Dragon talons tore into my skin and gorged out my heart to mark me – I didn't belong.

I was no one. In the darkness, screams of the fallen drowned out my cries of anguish, and no number of tears could erase the wound that lay festering and open at the core of my being.

'You have failed us,' my mother said as amber eyes conveyed her disappointment.

Her beautiful face contorted, changing into the most ferocious dragon I had ever seen before her mouth opened to devour me finally.

"Zataray," a voice called into the darkness.

My eyes fluttered. "What?" I answered, realizing it had all been just a dream.

My heart tightened inside my chest, though, while some tears escaped streaking down my face. I hadn't been able to escape the pain or stop the sobs that escaped my throat either.

A stunning face appeared before me, calling my name, "Zataray, I'm here. Hold on. I'm here," she said.

86

Finally, my senses came around, realizing that the voice that lent me strength and allowed me to hope was also the same voice that drew me toward shame all in one insinuating moment of awareness.

I closed my eyes before I spoke. "Go away," I said. My voice sounded harsher than I wanted it to be.

"You don't mean that – Silly," Nari chided me.

The Princess made a face at me as I opened one eye and pulled away to wipe at the wetness that told a story I would have liked to deny.

Nari had seen worse, but so had I. I turned to face her. "Why are you in my room, Princess?" I asked.

I wasn't fully awake to taunt Nari with her being so close to me, and I knew I didn't have to wait long for her reaction. She hated when I used her title against her.

On cue, Nari tensed. Her eyes narrowed into angry slits, and the breath in my lungs came out in one whoosh because I hadn't reacted in time to block the blow she had direct at my gut.

"What the Hell –"

"You know I hate it when you go there," Nari said and moved away from my bed.

I dragged my feet over the side and glanced sideways at her. The morning had just begun, and the sun rose to send its glare right into my eyes.

At least I hadn't wanted to believe that my reaction had been because Nari had dazzled me.

That had never happened before, and I didn't need it happening now. I know I was riled up about nothing, but I didn't want to admit that seeing Nari first thing when I opened my eyes made me want to take a cold shower.

And, the heat that ravaged me in the mornings was also growing worse. Was Nari the trigger?

"I don't know what you want," I said.

"I want you to stop beating yourself up over something that was never your fault. It's been three years, and you should be moving forward. And, you certainly shouldn't be dragging up things that were never under your control because it was never your fault," Nari concluded.

"I never thought for one moment it was my fault, Nari. You're so self-centered and conceited, Princess," I goaded her.

That got her going; her eyes flashed as she spun on me, expecting that my last retort was enough. Seriously who had I been trying to hurt with my remarks?

Both my hands were raised in protecting my head, as I expected that I had pushed Nari as far as I could when it came to baiting her into a fight.

She was also skilled at hand-to-hand combat even if I were the stronger, taller, and most likely to come out the winner.

I wasn't foolish enough to desire a fight because as mad and as riled up as she was now, Nari would crush me.

Nari hadn't hit me, which surprised me, and I looked her in the eyes before I glanced out the window – just past dawn.

"You should go back to bed," I said and made a friendly gesture as I patted my bed. "Unless you want to join me?" I asked.

"Zataray, you're such an Ass!" Nari retorted.

I noticed she had curled her slim fingers around her dagger.

She was dangerous even without the weapon she never left behind, carrying it always upon her person.

I took a good look at her under the golden filter of the rising sun. As intimidating when angry as Nari was, she was certainly drop-dead gorgeous as well.

Red-brown curls covered her head like sunrays in disarray, and her hazel eyes were expressive; it was hard not to get caught up if Nari paid attention to you.

And, even if she were the only girl that could drop kick you into tomorrow without messing her hair, she was also beautiful and kind to others – just not toward me.

Her drop-dead gorgeousness hadn't been enough to remove her tough bravado act, though. She hid a lot of her pain at not using magic behind it; maybe I hid a lot too; we were a lot alike.

Though staring at her now in the little bit of clothing she had on, it seemed to have gotten an unexpected reaction from me – Nari had affected me a lot lately.

Still, I just wasn't interested in her that way because we had practically adopted each other. Besides, all soldier's male and female, bathed in the same pool sometimes. So, I had seen plenty of naked bodies. Nari's nakedness wasn't anything special.

"What?" Nari asked, staring me in the eyes.

"Nothing. Just – go away!" I said as my voice rose. I was certain I just woke everyone else on the floor we shared.

I didn't even know why I felt so irritated. Nari always came to check on me every time I had nightmares. Today her checking on me had felt different somehow.

Whatever was burning inside of me just hadn't wanted to burn out or be subdued, and it was wearing me down.

I couldn't recall when Nari and I had started 'fighting' more than 'talking.' It was just too confusing to be around her anymore.

Still, Nari had a short memory. She appeared every single time I had dreams where my screams had probably woken the dead.

And every single time she arrived, I felt she had quieted the beast within me, but barely.

The door swung open and hit the wall with a bang.

"Hey, you two!" Mal hissed. The prince seemed more pissed off than Nari, which wasn't even possible.

"If you want to wake up the whole floor, then hit the training area!" he commanded.

"I'm going back to bed," I said as a yawn escaped before I could hold it back.

"Not an option, Warrior," Mal said.

I stared at Mal, deciding if I should rile both brother and sister so early in the morning. The odds weren't in my favor.

I threw my hands skyward. "Fine," I said, resolved I wasn't going to get much sleep anyways.

"Fine. See you in two heartbeats," Mal said before he eyed Nari up and down with a stare that could pierce clean through.

Mal shook his head in disgust. "Sheesh, Nari. Go put some clothes on," he said before he turned without a backward look and slammed the door making much more noise than I thought I had.

"Don't even say a word," Nari said without looking my way as she brushed past my bed.

I growled. "Trouble maker."

Nari shook her head. "If you want to talk about it – I'm here," she whispered. Her voice so low, I had to strain to understand her the last of her words.

She grasped the door handle and paused. I didn't speak, and she sighed, twisted the knob, and silently walked out, leaving the door ajar.

Yeah. Like I could just tell Nari how I loved the very two people that meant more than my life at present.

The very same two, I should be taking their life's blood to avenge my people's death.

I was frustrated, confused, and pissed that I had grown so weak. My 'beast' realized it. But, I couldn't see a future without Nari or Mal included in it.

'Sure, Princess – I have plenty I'd like to talk to you about,' I sent.

THE SCENT OF DISTRACTION

The training area wasn't a typical practice field, but when Mal made his appearance, the field narrowed even more to the point I felt claustrophobic.

Every soldier within the castle walls admired him, and the females flocked to him like he was the best thing since sliced bread.

Nari, on the other hand, seemed to have the opposite effect. Although she could have any guy she desires, young or old, she was brutal in training – a real shrew when it came to taking her anger out on anyone that challenged her abilities.

Nari was at the opposite end of the training area, and I could already feel the tension created by her presence – no one wanted to train with her.

I turned and observed Nari a little while longer than I should have. She was just so exciting to watch, especially when she trained.

No move was wasted, nor did she release any expanded energy; Nari was grace and beauty on the battlefield. Every action a calculated dance with death.

I realized that I could stare at her all day, but then I had a skill set to master my own.

I had always been a quick learner and had to prove my prowess several times since I was given a sword and asked to train as an Avidan warrior.

My muscle frame exuded the extent of arduous work and persistence; it also suggested that I loved this physical exertion.

I wanted to become even better than Mal. As strong as I've become, the Prince has had years of practice no matter how I bested others who tried to test my abilities.

91

Mal is still a prince, and I can only hope to become his second, but he has proven his station has not overshadowed his sense of right or his undying loyalty as a friend.

I may have suffered many misgivings, but I never regretted the friendship between Mal, Nari, and myself.

Since it's early than usual and no one has had time for breakfast, the general mood was beyond tense. I couldn't help but notice that Nari has moved into the arena with a few of her peers who were no match for her on even her worst days.

Since I've arrived, Nari has had her struggles as well; the outright disregard by the Elites who provoke her even here on the training fields is proof that I am not the only one they seek to humiliate daily.

The Elites' disregard of Nari Station hadn't gone unnoticed by Mal, who could have shown favoritism to his sister but hadn't. Every soldier must handle whatever is thrown at them and rise above even if they have royal blood or no.

Since Nari was the second born, she must prove her worth amongst the Avidan no matter her royal bloodline.

It seemed simple enough unless one didn't acquire the magic to gain the status of Wielder. A big deal to the royal bloodline of Avidan.

I believed it cruel and downright hurtful to be subjected to such idiot beliefs that could denounce your existence.

Nari may appear strong, confident, and stubborn as hell. Still, until she awakened her magic, the disregard of her station and the rampant disrespect that followed her would continue, and Mal won't interfere.

Nari had to endure, and as she always has done, even if it took every ounce of restraint within her – which isn't very much. Nari was destined for greatness, and she didn't need to prove that to a living soul.

Those same warriors should watch out, though. It wasn't Nari's fault that she hadn't come into her magic yet; it was only a matter of time. She made up for it with her kick-ass skills.

Some believed Nari would never wield magic, and some thought that she was Broken. A Magic Wielder who couldn't wield magic was considered the lowest, and the disrespect amongst peers was always unbearable.

The people of Avidan were heartless in their beliefs – I would know.

As a princess, Nari avoided the cruelty and outright disrespect of those in the upper class who were influential only because they feared the King's wrath, but more so than that, they hadn't wanted to face Mal's retaliation.

His sister was the only one he cared about; I knew that it didn't fare well for those who outwardly disrespected her when he was near.

There was no way that Nari could be Broken; she was fierce, beautiful, and royalty – and at times a royal pain.

Still, Nari was honest to a fault, and what mean streak she possessed seemed reserved for the likes of me. Nari, unlike her father, seemed devoid of the cruelty. The Kingdom's belief hadn't rubbed off on either of the royal siblings and for that, I was alive, a benefactor of their combined kindness.

Everyone waits in anticipation for Nari's powers to awaken as the Shamans had disclosed, but it had been years since that foretelling, and nothing has happened to prove them correct. While others grew impatient, no telling what would happen if, upon her eighteenth birthday, the princess could harness her magic.

Nari didn't have the luxury of time on her side.

Her eighteenth birthday was close; I wasn't as hopeful as I pretended to be about her success rate either.

The clang of metal against metal pulled me from my negative thoughts. Regardless, this morning would probably be no different for Nari or me as we still had to show strength while struggling with doubt.

Those who wished her well and those who hope she fails to follow her every footstep as they wait in anticipation when that moment might arise.

Look! As if just my thoughts had become a tangible thing; the crowds have arrived, pacing straight for the training grounds, seemingly bound to see for themselves if Nari would break through her curse and become what her bloodline demanded of her.

Only, I knew their appearance caused Nari grief.

It was also strange that those same naysayers had never affected me one way or the other. My worth was never measured by their censure or disdain that I am 'kept' amongst the royals as a former slave to their now extinct enemies. Unaware that there is still one enemy that remains to remember every slight and stare from their hate-filled eyes.

I've long ago dispelled the whispering of those who questioned who I was. No one had a clue about 'What I am' because it would scare them silly.

Only the King, the king's captain, Nari, and Mal knew my identity. As far as everyone was concerned, I was a servant to the Prince with special privileges.

Still, my uniqueness stood out like a sore thumb. My looks alone confirmed I wasn't of Avidan descent.

My background remained questionable because my appearance was nothing like these brown skin people with lean builds. I was taller, broader, and fairer skin, but my hair and eye color proved even more that I was from another place. I was born to a people of a different race. My hair and eyes were silver.

Luckily, no one has seen my kind that might connect me with the Dragonshifter's, or I might not be alive to live amongst them as I do.

Time hasn't changed their hatred even after three years; I'm shunned because I don't belong. At least I would like to believe that is the extent of it. Even among the Elites, I remain unwelcomed, although my skills could easily rank near the top next to Mal and Nari.

I had no friends amongst them, but I shared an unbreakable bond with the King's son and daughter, so I was tolerated. I wasn't disillusioned about who I was just because I got to hang out with the Prince and Princess of Avidan.

I was an outsider and remained uncertain if I wished to claim an affinity toward people who had slaughtered my family.

Still, I was afforded a chance to prove these same people wrong about their beliefs about shifters being 'vile creatures were.'

Also, I realized I had issues as well; If only I were courageous enough to go against the King's gag order condemning my existence or connection to a people he has ordered slain to extinction.

I remained silenced by an unknown hand that restrained me from claiming my rightful identity. There was nothing honorable about my living amongst the Avidans.

Still, I don't believe I can question my two closest friends' loyalty.

No matter how much we all irritate the hell out of each other – we share something special.

"Stop daydreaming and get some work in," Mal said as he nailed me good with a right hook.

"Dammit, Mal!" I retorted as I rubbed the left side of my jaw, drew back my shoulder, and swung my sword arm back and then forth.

I wasn't about to let Mal get away with catching me off guard either.

"I thought you'd be taking on someone your own size," I goaded my best friend.

"Naw. I thought I'd pick on someone weaker than me," Mal said.

I winced. He could be vicious when he was ticked off, which seemed a lot lately.

"What's got you riled up?" I asked as I countered his sword thrust with a jab toward his ribcage to give me some breathing room.

"Nari's at it again, and I have to let her figure it out. I want to wring their necks – and hers," Mal grunted as he countered my attack.

I dropped my guard and tilted my head back as I bellowed out a laugh, "Fat chance!" I said.

"The only thing about that which isn't funny is that those fools will need a Shaman's healing after Nari's finished with them," I breathed out.

I actually felt in a better mood and commented as much, "Better them than me," I said.

"You'd think she'd be used to it by now," Mal shifted his eyes as he glanced back at his sister. I felt his ire and helplessness at his inability to help her.

I shrugged and decided I couldn't think about Nari because she gave me a headache. I swept at Mal's feet to unbalance him and gain an advantage.

Mal jumped back and pointed his sword in my direction before he focused his attention on me.

"Tsk–tsk, Little Brother, I've taught you better than this," Mal said as his smile wasn't even remotely a sign that he was feeling anything other than irritated.

Besides, when Mal got this upset about Nari, I realized that I was the one that suffered.

I was in for the worst of ass-kicking since Mal couldn't go to Nari's rescue.

The muscles tightened in my jaw, even as I attempted to breathe in and then out.

"Fine. Let's do this!" I said as a slow smile formed on my face.

It hadn't stopped my gut from tightening, though. Nothing could fix the unease that settled over me when I thought about Nari and why I had been reacting strangely whenever she was near.

Facing Mal like this was going to be bad.

And, to prove my prediction, Mal hit me twice in the face and then targeted my gut with a high kick that sent me flying backward.

I straightened my frame and shrugged.

"Let's get this over with," I said, no longer smiling.

CHAPTER SIX – NARI

SCATTERED EMOTIONS

The heat from the pool settled into my bones and cooled my anger. Kneading at the tightness in my arms and legs helped too.

It had been a while since I went all out on the practice field, but the tears that threatened had me discombobulated, and I cursed the circumstance that made me feel so damn vulnerable.

Why did I let my sparing partners goad me? I shouldn't have allowed them to get under my skin, but I had.

It was no use pretending that I wasn't riled up about it; raising my hands to eye level, I wiggled my fingers in the hope that I could sense magic stir inside me. I wanted to feel anything, even if it were just a tingling sensation that would suggest that I could magic wield.

I got nothing.

My mother had reminded me that a Magic Wielder's power wasn't something that could be pinned down as to when the gift would arrive, only that it 'should.'

Yet, signs of our ability to use magic always appeared between the fifteenth and sixteenth years of birth.

And, I had already turned eighteen.

Each Wielder was different. I knew this, but it still didn't stop me from desiring my gift sooner than later, especially since I had become the brute of everyone's teasing.

My wielder's power would appear in its own timing, or at the time of my greatest need, my mother had attempted to console me.

But wasn't my greatest need now?

At eighteen, I was expected to take on a battalion of my own, like Mal. Until I could prove my abilities to wield magic, I was as useless as any servant that roamed the halls of my castle home.

I definitely couldn't protect any placed in my command. Without successfully honing my skills, I would have to depend on my brother. I was nothing more than an embarrassment and liability.

Broken. That is what my people called me behind my back. And, for some reason, it bothered me. I was a princess of Avidan; it shouldn't have mattered, but it did.

More tears surged forth while I sunk deeper into the pool to cover my despair.

"I would have never thought I'd see the day the Little Princess would cry," a male voice spoke behind me.

I didn't even turn my head to acknowledge Zataray as I continued to soak in the heated pool.

"I told you – stop calling me 'Princess!' I retorted, taking my feeling sorry for myself out on my friend. "Why does it matter what I do, Zataray?" I asked. I couldn't even muster enough energy even to argue.

I had spent all my anger out on the training field, now all I wanted was peace to wallow, and Zataray had ruined even that.

Zataray didn't respond right away as he removed his gear and discarded his clothing to step into the pool opposite where I sat.

His eyes met mine, staring me down like he wanted to throttle me.

"What did I do now?" I asked. The last thing I wanted to do was argue or pick a fight, which seemed about all we could do as of late.

"It's just funny to me, Princess. You don't seem the type to bother with other people's opinions – what has happened?" he asked.

"Nothing," I mumbled my reply because Zataray was right.

Only what triggered me seemed unavoidable, and I couldn't 'act' as though I was okay because I hadn't been in a long time.

My mind felt flooded by wayward emotions lately, and it hadn't been all about my inability to hone magic either; I just couldn't put my finger on it.

My eyes sought my friend's gray eyes before I lowered my gaze, wishing I were anywhere else but next to Zataray.

"What's up?" Zataray asked.

I shook my head, refusing to look his way. "Nothing."

"Bull –

"You don't have to be crude!" I interrupted him.

Zataray eyed me for a minute before he reached for a sponge, "I'm not a talker – so figure it out on your own," he said.

"You're a Jerk," I said out of habit and closed my eyes, sinking further into the heated pool.

I sighed through my frustration, wondering what had gotten into me; I wasn't myself at all.

Zataray's laughter filtered across the pool and irked me to no end.

I tossed my head up and responded. "You're smug, high and mighty, and a servant who should know his place," I said the last part under my breath.

I must have hit a nerve because Zataray pointed at me. "And, you're conceited, a Know-it-all and a Shrew," he said.

The Shrew part stung but, even I knew I could be difficult to get along with at times.

It was a defense mechanism to hide the pain that I felt every day that I couldn't help Zataray with his nightmares or myself facing the knowledge that I might be – Broken.

I was shaking by the time I responded to his calling me a shrew.

"You should go to Master Teacher's class then. Maybe he'll teach you to be a 'Know-it-all' and a Shrew too!" I retorted and slid back into the heated water; only I slid too deep.

Grabbing hold of the edge of the pool, I pulled myself upright, but not before I choked when the water went up into my nose, which stung as I coughed to clear my passage.

I expected to hear Zataray's laughter, but he wasn't laughing at all as he looked at me.

"If you let them question your power, you will lose your way – you're better than any of them," he said in a quiet tone to where I almost had to strain to hear.

"You have no idea what it's like," I countered and looked down at my hands before I found enough courage to look into his eyes once more. Eyes that appeared so damn beautiful that I couldn't stop staring, and then our gaze connected.

I shook my head. "That's not fair," I said. "I just meant...it's been three years and – nothing."

I held up my hands to emphasize my meaning. Suddenly, tears stormed past my defenses, and I swiped at my eyes, but it was too late to stop them.

I felt mortified that I wasn't strong, and I watched the wet drops of my shame drip onto the surface of the pool. The person I wanted everyone to see hadn't come to the surface in a long time. It was often just me alone with my doubts and fears.

I knew it wasn't easy for me to share my feelings, but Zataray had always been willing to listen during the times when we weren't angry at each other. Half the time? I didn't understand why I was pushing him away.

I wasn't behaving like myself at all, and losing my composure was so demeaning. Besides, I couldn't deny Zataray's claims. I found myself acting just like Zataray described – spiteful and mean.

"It's okay," Zataray said.

Before I could form a thought or respond, Zataray was by my side; his eyes never left mine.

"You are none of those things I just called you, Nari. What you are is special. Everyone knows it. It would help if you believed that too," Zataray said as his words reached me, and his breath tickled my ear.

My body reacted; it felt like the first time I met Zataray almost three years ago – like I was drowning.

My heart raced, my breath seemed caught in my throat, even though I tried to swallow without bringing attention to the fact that Zataray's face was like two inches from mine.

I was rather good at denial, it seemed.

My eyes shot to his. It was like being drawn into a cloud the color of silver – had he always been so beautiful?

I was acutely aware of his broad shoulders that hovered close to mine; neither of us had an inch of clothing on.

It was as if an invisible string drew us together, connecting us. I couldn't stop my gaze from lowering to his mouth either; it was slightly open, or Zataray's hot breath caressed my face.

Heat also shot through my core, and I clenched my hands to keep them from roaming all over Zataray's bare skin.

What was wrong with me?

My eyes wanted to devour all of him at once, but the draw was real – the hypnotic pull, intense.

I felt frightened. *'Was what I felt some sort of power transfer that Dragon Shifters possessed?'*

It was as if I was held in place by an invisible vice, and an unknown force was feeding off my emotions like Zataray was inside my mind.

Still, I hadn't been weirded out by the experience more so; it felt more like I desired it. And I attempted to console the fact that I felt this way because I had been blindsided – it wasn't my fault that my heartbeat like a drum inside my chest as his arm touched mine.

'Oh my God, he looks at me like I'm his.'

There was a part of me that believed it was possible; hell, I wouldn't even be able to deny it.

Neither one of us has broken the silence or moved until I noticed that our lips lowered, closing the impossible space that held us apart.

I hadn't thought to break the silence or shatter the moment between us – ever.

It's the closest I've ever felt to Zataray. It felt like all of our emotions had been upended, sabotaged, and molded into something altogether different than either one of us had expected – something unforeseen.

Our lips drew closer, and I closed my eyes, but someone coughed, and we both jumped apart.

"I wonder if you two have absorbed all the heat out of the pool yet?"

I swore that magic was involved at that moment but, the spell ended, and Zataray pushed himself away to end up where he was before whatever it was that drew up together happened.

I reached for whatever connection that I could reform; my eyes sought him out, but Zataray didn't look at me at all.

Sighing, I turned my head to acknowledge my brother.

"Come on in, it's still hot," I said.

CHAPTER SEVEN – ZATARAY

THE FIRE BENEATH

Fresh, freezing morning air hit me square in the face, but it didn't do the job it was supposed to.

The heat that rampaged within my veins was far from being quenched.

Winter was almost here, and maybe the cold could help me focus – perhaps not.

So far, it hadn't done me a bit of good, and I was restless. For the last six days, I had succumbed to a routine that I could live with – fight, eat, bathe, sleep.

Oh yeah, I needed to mention the fight part; Mal's has been kicking my butt worse than ever.

To think that I believed I was getting better than him now seems laughable. And, sleeping is impossible for any length of time without the nightmares that followed.

Training alone in the wee hours of the morning is about the only thing that can settle my ire. It hasn't been too bad, and I enjoyed the peace that dropped over Avidan just before the sun rose.

My ability to focus on perfecting my skill and hiding my gift seemed futile; sooner or later, I did not doubt that my fate would be handed to me when I found out about the latter.

So, I pushed myself even harder, but not even when I fueled my workouts with fresh anger did it soothe the heat that burned my veins. My efforts were wasted as soon as the mental picture of a certain Princess's lips met mine. It doused my focus like a bucket full of ice.

'Damn,' when did I start thinking about her in that way?'

There was only one solution; I made it a habit to avoid Nari as if she carried the plague. Facing her wasn't an option. No matter the darkness that pulled me deeper into the 'dreams' that seemed alive and malevolent.

The very thought of the existence of my fears seemed to attach to a part of my soul in which I couldn't rid myself of the feeling that I was losing myself.

The darkness came more frequent and more insistent since I had shut Nari away.

Nari knew how to bring me back from that despair but, I had been stubborn and locked my door at night. I hadn't allowed her the opportunity to 'save' me.

Once I had thought about it, though, Nari wouldn't allow a locked door to stand in the way unless she, too, had been avoiding me.

If only I had a chance in hell, she desired to be with me, but she doesn't want me. I couldn't believe how defeated I felt.

I never thought I'd become such a coward, but I can't face the fact that all I wanted to do was take the princess in my arms and kiss her when I looked at her.

Damn. Nari was practically like a sister to me. How could this happen? I pressed the balls of my palms into my forehead, attempting to rid the look in her eyes just before I tried to kiss her.

She looked pissed.

Was I that despicable of a person to her? The Half-blood good enough to call a friend and 'brother,' but that's the extent of it, huh?

It was laughable if I weren't so damn sure I would still risk her wrath just to wrap her up in my arms – daggers on her person be damned.

'Nari. Damn it – get out of my head!'

Day six, and she hasn't as much come to find me either. She avoided the practice field when I was there and the baths too. Fine! I couldn't care if we spoke two words to each other ever again.

"Happy now?" Mal asked. He had just finished kicking me around the training area like I was chopped wood.

"I have no idea what you mean," I in response, I attempted to reassert myself getting in a good shot while Mal was preoccupied.

I missed as he ducked and countered with another blow to my ribs.

"Damn it, Zataray! If your heads not in the game, you'll wind up mincemeat. Calm your blood, Brother – seek your inner fire," Mal reminded me as he proceeded to give me a few more bruises.

Twenty minutes later, I held up my hand and called it quits.

My 'Inner Fire' had all but been drained away. It was a personal reference between him, Nari, and me.

It had also been our secret. I only told the two of them that my blood burned hot sometimes. And it hadn't been a normal heat either.

'It's your Dragon half,' Mal had informed me, and Nari agreed.

Something that didn't matter since I knew I couldn't shift anyways because I was only a half-dragon and not a full-blooded Shifter.

Besides, Nari told me a long time ago that the only reason I was alive was that that 'part of me' would never awaken.

As much as Nari believed that she was Broken because she held no ability to use magic, I had felt just as 'Broken'; my abilities to fully utilize my inherent right as a Shifter was just as unattainable.

"No use hiding," Mal pokes me with the butt end of his sword, "The only reason you think you're able to avoid Nari is that she's avoiding you too," Mal laughs, "I can't believe that you didn't kiss her."

"I'm not hiding, and I wasn't about to kiss her in the first place!" I retrieved my sword and stormed off to find a good cold pool to soothe my heated blood.

Lately, my symptoms had gotten worse. In the past, only Nari has been able to 'cool' me down when I would wake from my nightmares or become agitated.

Most times, though, Nari had been the instigator of my anger, and yet my blood never boiled beyond control when we argued. I never questioned why that was so until now.

Before I could make it to the baths, Captain Jeril appeared with a mock bow, "Half-blood," he said quietly as he addressed me.

I stiffened at his intended insult but showed no other sign that his label of my ancestry has affected me.

"Captain," I said.

"You've grown stronger; I hope you find the King's mercy satisfactory?" he asked.

What did he mean, *'Satisfactory?'*

I attempted to be civil, but it was harder than I thought when I replied. "Captain, it's rare that you speak to me at all. Am I being called to be administered over so soon?" I asked.

I couldn't even manage to keep the sarcasm from creeping into my voice.

"Half-blood, you have no idea," Captain Jeril replied, and without uttering another word, he turned, expecting that I follow.

"Zataray!" Mal called after me.

He had run to catch up to the captain and me, but I could already sense that he was pissed.

"Is he to go to my father or the mages?" Mal asked.

"You, Sir Prince, do not get to question the King, not by a long shot – know your place, Prince."

"I will remember to do just that, Captain Jeril," Mal replied.

I noticed Mal tense up, but he managed to show a side of him that wouldn't place me in further danger and became the 'well-mannered' Prince.

I almost laughed at his attempt to do so; both the captain and I knew better.

The only tell-tale sign that Mal was seething inside had been the look in his eyes; his left twitched – not good.

I hated what was to happen next but, I should have been used to it by now. I had to face the inquisitors.

Would I live to see another day, or would I be condemned to death – it was time to go before the Shaman and be tested.

CHAPTER EIGHT – NARI

MAKE WAR – NOT LOVE

"Mal!" I called out to my brother, "What's going on? The whole place is buzzing," I asked, running up to him out of breath.

"Father's calling the Counsel together," he says, but his eyes hold anger I've never seen before, and I can sense there's something he's not saying.

"We haven't any more Dragons to kill – so who are we fighting?"

"I don't know everything, Nari – you're to be there, so we'll both find out at the same time," Mal retorted.

"Touchy much? I asked, ignoring my brother's obvious mood. "So...where's Zataray?"

Mal stopped and looked me straight in the eyes; he looked like he wanted to strangle me.

"It's been a week, and you haven't spoken to 'our brother' or mentioned his name. Hell, Nari, you couldn't even tell that he was sent to be tested again by our father and the Mages, have you?" Mal asked. His anger wasn't directed at me, but I backed up anyway.

I shook my head, "I'm no Magic Wielder like you, Mal – how was I supposed to know?" I asked.

Although, I did feel something wasn't right. I looked past my brother, guilty that he hit the nail on the head.

'Zataray needed me, and I was busy playing the blame game.' I grasped my brother's arm, "I was scared, Mal." I pleaded with him to understand. "If Father were even to guess –

"You'd better become unafraid then because they're coming after you next, Nari – why the hell can't you hide your feelings?" Mal asked.

"You know – he doesn't even like me that way," I said. At least I hadn't thought that he had.

"Everybody that has any sense can tell you've both fallen for each other – don't fool yourself," Mal said.

"I don't...he couldn't possibly – I can't be," I stuttered, unable to put two words together coherently.

"Deny all you want, I'll do my best to hide you behind a Truth Veil, but you two better get your act together. We're all expected to lead our soldiers, and there's no way in hell Father's going to allow a relationship to happen between you two. Damn it, Nari – why now? When all Zataray can do is hide his Blood Fire from the mages," Mal said.

"He's got it under control," I said. "I hope."

Mal's eyes studied me for a moment. His eyes conveyed a lot. Mostly his disappointment.

"Because of you, Nari – he doesn't," Mal replied.

"What do I do?" I asked, almost near tears. It wouldn't do for anyone to see me so messed up. But what if what Mal said was true?

"Deny your love for him. Deny it to Father so that 'our beloved' Father believes you but, most of all, deny it to Zataray so much so that 'our brother' will have no choice but to hate you for it," Mal said, offering a solution.

Tears well up in my eyes. "Okay," I said.

Now wasn't the time to be timid or weak. I nodded my head, "Alright, I'll do it," I said.

I had to pull it off. Zataray's life hung by the thread of my deception – I was surprisingly good at tossing lies about it seemed.

Mist covered the hillside and camouflaged soldiers and horses alike.

The fog wasn't normal; the weather seemed aided by those who controlled the atmosphere – something I should be able to do if I possessed magic.

"This war was bound to happen," Mal whispered. We were huddled together near the frontline; Mal squatted next to me from watching the battalion's movements.

"Once the other Kingdoms realized that Father had taken no prisoners but committed genocide as far as the Dragon shifters were concerned, there's no coming to the outrage," he said.

I nodded. "Even years later, I get the sense that when he doomed their women and children, there would be consequences, but a full-out war?" I asked.

"It's more than just the Dragonshifter's, Nari. This unrest has been building for a long time; no one can stomach a tyrant without consequences. It was bound to happen," Mal said.

"I just don't want to see our people caught up, but there's no hope for it. I heard rumors – they're afraid of your magic," I said.

"No," Mal shook his head as he eyed me. "They're afraid of your magic, Nari."

I started. "I have no magic, Mal. Everyone knows it."

"Not yet," he said and spun about as he looked over his shoulder. "Be careful if anything looks like trouble get your high-tail it back to me, is that clear?" he commanded.

I nodded. "On it!" I said as I thought about something else. "Will our sister Kingdom, Zatius, take a stand with us?" I asked.

"If they uncovered that Zataray was related to their people or if any of our own realized that we kept a half-blood alive, we'd be fighting with our own in rebellion – let them come against us. We are the stronger army," Mal retorted.

I nodded, but my eyes trailed after a single figure who had separated from our ranks.

"Time to go see what advantages are to be had. Want to go and see if we can end this quickly, Nari?" Mal asked.

I shook my head, yes. No one was better at deception than Zataray and me, especially since we couldn't 'perform' magic. We learned to be better, quicker, more adept at countering magic than any other.

"What's he doing?" I pointed at Zataray, who had taken a position near the bottom of the hill. Just as I also realized that he was going off on his own.

I started to rise and go after him, but Mal grabbed at my arm to halt me.

"Zataray has his own set of instructions – don't interfere, Nari. Just find a way through the pass without us losing any more soldiers. Do your duty," my brother's words bite deep.

I wasn't certain, but Mal knew how much I loved Zataray; he always protected me. But if I wanted to go after my best friend, nothing was going to stop me.

"Focus, Sis," Mal stared me down.

I nodded. Mal already knew I'd throw everything away just to save the boy with the silver eyes.

"Nari, get a grip!" Mal retorted, which brought my focus back to him.

"I'm not going after him!" I said as I reached for my dagger and slipped around our soldiers to find a way past our enemies.

My mind reeled from yesterday's events when I informed Zataray that I had no intentions of pursuing anything between us. In fact, I had also reminded him that I found 'desiring' a Half-blood was beneath my station as a Princess of Avidan.

'You're such a Conceited Shrew.' Zataray reminded me.

'And, you're still a Servant – know your place,' I reminded him.

'Yes, it's all about knowing where one belongs that gives one the edge. Don't worry, Princess; my 'place' is already a given.'

I'm sure there was a double meaning hidden in his statement. Knowing Zataray, he was so good at hiding behind his wall of darkness that even if I did confess that it was all a lie about how I felt, he would still throw salt into the wound just to injure me further.

I also stopped attempting to deny that I loved him so much that I could barely breathe – he'd laugh in my face.

I was utterly hopeless – I couldn't save Zataray. I couldn't even save myself.

"Hurry back, Sis," Mal said as I waved off his concern.

I had become a much better soldier than my first scrimmage three years ago.

I disappeared into the hazy grayness of the Mage Mist.

My mind wandered, though, as I thought about Zataray. Neither of us could deny that this 'separation' caused us both to be somewhat off our game – how could it not?

Going out alone was dangerous, and we both needed all our focus on making it back alive. Because when Zataray did make it back, I was going to cuss him out and give him the beat down, 'Royally.'

Three years had come and gone; I hoped that I had grown up a little, even if it were just to be I've grown up a little, even if it's just to be reminded how cruel a could be to ones who had no control over their fate.

I knew denying my love for Zataray could wound my soul irrevocably. Had he felt the same?

Shifting my train of thought back to my task wasn't all that difficult as I passed the telltale signs of war.

I was staggered by the amount of death that I witnessed firsthand, and because of my profession, I would witness repeatedly.

Three years to grow so close to a boy with silver eyes with a heart that begs eternally for forgiveness for something that was never his fault.

We spent three years building a trust forged with a common bond that connected us whether we wanted it or not.

And, it had also been three years since the Shaman stated that I would come into my power as a Magic Wielder, while the same time passed us by in which Zataray was supposed to help me attain that goal.

And now, we had come full circle and faced war yet again, all for the sake of Avidan's people and its belief regarding magic.

It was just too much; I feared the war would always be our way of life. My father reveled in it. He didn't care who he destroyed because of it.

Who would Avidan direct their hatred at next; who would get singled out for extermination? I wasn't even certain that my Father's justice was even considered justice.

But, I was certain that the aftermath of his actions resulted in the retaliation that our people must face.

And, it hadn't been swift enough in its coming. I almost wished that Zataray would take this moment to run – to flee Avidan and never look back.

'Zataray – run! Never look back. Don't think about me ever again!'

I sniffed, chiding my inability to hide my despair; my feelings had nothing to do with securing a means through our enemy lines;

I had to focus, or I needed explanations as to why I was even out here?

On my hands and knees, I slowed the pace to a snail's crawl, barely moving. I wasn't even certain when I understood that we were way over our heads, but an enemy encampment in our territory wasn't what I had expected.

The magic felt oddly familiar, and I was drawn toward it even though my mind was awhirl. Worried about falling into enemy hands should have been a priority, but it wasn't.

My heart was doing a number on me as I remembered the look in Zataray's eyes as I trod on any hopes that our friendship could become more.

I wanted one last honest talk with him, though, at least to remind him that I am no one to care about and especially not someone he could ever love; he deserved someone other than a coward. Maybe it was better that we ended our friendship with a war between us.

My cowardice act only gave Zataray pain; I gave him nothing to hold on to other than darkness.

To love someone like me could only end in disaster anyway. I was Broken, after all.

CHAPTER NINE – NARI

THE CONJURING

The night was transforming into dawn, and I couldn't determine how far I had traveled away from the main army, but it was far.

Stranger still, I hadn't located any signs that the enemy was close by – something wasn't right.

I felt as though I had been running around in circles and couldn't get past the fact that magic surrounded me.

The withdrawing moon hid behind cloud cover, and even though the mist had dissipated, I was hidden well enough – if only Zataray were here.

What am I saying? There was no way he would come to assist Mal or me, not after what I said. Zataray didn't deserve the sorry excuses I used to turn him away.

My heart grieved at the way it was handled. But Mal had been right. If Zataray believed I was available to pursue, he wouldn't have given up on me so easily.

I had to make certain he knew I wasn't interested. Not in the least – not one bit.

I reached up and touched my lips, imagining the kiss that almost took place at the pool. I had wanted him to kiss me.

Ugh! "Focus on the mission," I whispered to myself.

Mal would be all over me if I failed him because I had been thinking about a Shifter.

I didn't blame Mal, and I knew he thought of Zataray like a younger brother, which made it awkward to have stronger feelings that involved kissing.

I'm the one that must face the music or the sword if I failed our father in this, though, not Mal, and certainly not Zataray.

Something moved to my right, thankful that I caught sight of it before I stepped out of my hiding place.

What was Zataray doing this far out? Had he followed me?

I thought Mal said he had a different mission.

I decided that I was going to scrape the rest of my scoping out the area.

'Mal was going to kill me.'

"What are you after, Zataray?" I asked into the stillness of the night as if it would answer me.

For a full hour, I trailed behind Zataray. On several occasions, my instinct screamed at me that something wasn't quite right. I wanted to make Zataray aware of my presence but, something stopped me.

'An intuitive warning?'

I hit the ground and snaked through the grasses in stealth mode, quite certain that Zataray was well aware that he was no longer alone.

Let's just hope he didn't double back and stab me in the back before I could identify myself.

After a few more moments of following Zataray, I could see lights flickering off and on between the seams of a massive artificially constructed wall of magic – found you!

"And, look what has fallen into the wolf's den?" A voice said somewhat off to my left. "Not a rabbit but a Princess."

I didn't jump up right away until I conceded that I was pretty much surrounded on three sides.

A simple conjuring illusion. So that was what I was stuck in. The enemy could be right next to our main army, and this...spell had been simple enough to trap me.

I had lost my focus thinking about Zataray – Mal tried to warn me.

I was okay with it, and I wasn't about to admit my mistake either. I had found what I was looking for, and hopefully, the message I sketched into a tiny bit of Mal's concealed magic would be enough of a warning; he would see what I saw.

"Look, I don't deny I was spying but, all's fair in war," I said as I stood with raised hands in the air.

"Funny, you should say that," another voice said.

I jerked about, my eyes glued on the speaker as my hand dove for my dagger, ready to pierce the speaker's heart.

"Hi, Princess."

My heart pounded inside my chest. "I told you don't call me Princess!" I retorted.

All this time, Mal and I protected Zataray's ass which was even more painful for me to stomach because now he stood leering at me. He had run, after all. Straight to the enemy to join them.

"The enemy of my enemy that was once my friend," I said.

CHAPTER TEN – NARI

IN THE FACE OF THINE ENEMIES

I had not been gagged or bound but, it was only after my captures threatened to tie me up like a hog if I didn't stop acting like a wild beast.

I finally relented as I followed Zataray and my enemies into their camp on the other side of the manufactured wall – It was impressive.

After I had seen to my needs, I was allowed to bathe and dress. Two guards pretended disinterest when I exited the tent, but I felt their stares upon my back.

I was non the less allowed to walk freely, as I was led to another enclosure that screamed 'luxury,' and I wondered how long they had been in Avidan's backyard.

Inside I found more clothing, my dagger, and sheath,

'Daring me much?'

A female poked her head into the tent, "The leaders wait for you, Princess," she said.

Part of me wanted to tell her where her precious 'leaders' could wait, but I was too curious about my captors to spoil the moment.

When I entered a large tent, a banquet of such enormity was spread before me that my stomach betrayed me and growled hungrily at the table-laden feast.

A lone figure watched me; his eyes bore into me, and I tensed as I observed him as well; he was someone important.

He was a foreigner, tall, dark hair, and built like a beast ready to fight. His eyes held mine, and he shifted his stance to greet me as I neared the center of the room.

Several rows of wealthy men were seated to our left and right, 'fed' by women in scantily dressed clothing, much like what I had been subjected to wear.

I glanced down at my outfit – very slutty. It didn't even have a sheath for my knives.

The stranger's eyes pierced straight through me; they devoured me even. It was as if I were no more than food to a starving man, and with eyes downcast, I stood stock still – the demure Princess had made an appearance.

When I finally dared to look up, he gestured for me to take a seat next to his side.

"Do my Father's enemies wish to use me as ransom? It won't work – he would kill me himself if he could. I am no use to you," I said as I cut to the chase.

"Does she always speak this boldly," A bearded man with light brown hair glanced over at Zataray, who had his hands full.

A female server has her bosom almost near his face as she poured him wine.

He waited for her to hand him his cup before he leaned across the torso of another scantly clad female and addressed the bearded man.

"She is mean-spirited and mouthy," he answers.

I was appalled at Zataray's nonchalant attitude.

"And, you're a traitor!" I stated the obvious and shut my mouth before letting loose a tirade of curses that I felt he deserved.

Zataray bowed before me.

"I told you, Princess – I am your enemy. I will always be so. I have no love for your father or his beliefs; I'm just returning the favor," he said.

I shook with disbelief. "I had nothing to do with it!" I shouted.

"You who came into my home covered in blood – the blood of my family! You are no better than your father or your brother!" Zataray said as he reminded me of my many faults.

"Leave Mal out of it," I retorted. "Mal loves you like his flesh and blood brother," I whispered as I got my emotions back under control.

'*I loved you much more than that.*' I almost cried but held back my tears and tried to compose myself before so many strangers.

They only seemed amused by the show.

"Now, now, Princess — we eat first, then maybe we argue or not?" The dark, imposing stranger interrupted Zataray and me.

"What are you expecting to gain out of all of this," I finally asked the dark man with effort. I had regained my composure and straightened to prove it.

"If I may, Princess Arnari," The man with the dark eyes bowed toward me.

"We merely wish for the King of Avidan to give up his throne and release the many prisoners that he 'hasn't' killed. We have it on competent authority that he holds them imprisoned in your very dungeons," he said.

"Why would my father keep such abominations?" I cringed at my words; I didn't believe that the Shifters were any different than those of my people who used magic but, Zataray had me spitting mad — I couldn't wait to cut his heart out.

"Tsk, Tsk, Princess. Such condescending viewpoints are no longer acceptable in our Kingdom, and Zatius stands with us — as does this young man and his unfortunate detainment from returning to his rightful place as a Prince of Zatius," he said.

My head snapped around to meet Zataray's eyes. Was he a Prince?

I didn't catch everything, but I returned my focus near the end of the dark stranger's words.

Was I in shock? The new information about Zataray's royal connection had gagged me far better than any mouthpiece ever could.

"...they only wish for their prince to return. I hear a hefty sum of money is offered as a reward for his safe return. The King's daughter a victim of your Father's quest to purge the Kingdom of Shifters, I understand. Of course, we as friends to Zatius and do not require compensation unless it's for their army to join our side against your father," he said.

I shook my head. "What?"

"We also hope to rescue what appears to be the last of its kind, a Half-blood Dragon Shifter. And, it is a widely known fact that 'your' Father keeps a Half-blood in bondage," he replied.

I glanced over at Zataray and then back at the man with the beard – he didn't know.

"And, you want to trade me for the Shifter? My father would rather kill him and me than allow him to live amongst us," I said. The last part was the truth, and I hoped I sounded convincing.

"He will come around."

"And can I know your name?" I asked the man with the dark skin, hair, and eyes that reflect like onyx gems in the torches' light. They also reveal silent insanity just underneath his calm façade. Now wasn't the time to play words with this man.

"I'm Tarn Luzon, the Chief Commander," he introduced himself with a flourished bow while his eyes continued to devour me.

I've never felt such intensity from anyone like Tarn Luzon before; I feel underdressed and vulnerable even with my dagger on my person.

My eyes go back to Zataray's, whose eyes have narrowed to the point that I became acutely aware that he could pounce on Tarn Luzon and pulverize him.

'What's got him so riled up?'

He has also remained unusually quiet throughout the whole of the commander chief's interrogation.

'Stupid, Princess, can't you follow your brother's orders? Why did you follow me?'

It only took a moment as I shook my head and envisioned sticking my tongue out at Zataray in my mind's eye.

'Had Zataray just spoke into my thoughts?

"I can show you better ways to use that,' he sent to me, which caused me to blush.

'I'll hold your little secret – for now!' I retorted back in the same way he communicated with me.

I had grown numb with grief. There was no way my father would exchange my life for Zataray's.

Which seemed quite the conundrum. Zataray was already inside the enemy's clutches – what a mess. The commander hadn't even realized that he wouldn't have to ransom me away at all.

Then with a commotion, I watched as Zataray excused himself from the room. Whatever game that the Shifter is playing, I hope that he can somehow include me – I was at a loss.

I glanced up in time to see the commander's eyes narrow as he watched after Zataray's departure before settling back on me.

'Damn.'

CHAPTER ELEVEN – ZATARAY

THE RESCUE

'So – Damn – Hot,' I groaned and rolled over. It had to be early dawn but, I felt like I haven't slept in three days. I couldn't get the freaking image of the princess out of my mind.

"Damn Nari," I cursed her. "What am I doing?" I asked no one. Nothing had gone according to plan since Nari's capture. If I continued to freak out like this, I would give away my cover too.

I had several questions for the commander, too. Only, the more I spoke with Luzon, the more I shifted my ideals that resonated with his way of thinking – we were of like-minds.

He believed that he could sway its ruler to lay down its belief that they were superior to others. And, that magic wasn't something coveted to maintain power, but the magic had to be shared so that civilizations could thrive.

'Find a way to cut off the head from the inside,' the King had ordered. *'And, your freedom to leave this country is granted but, you may never return.'* He had made it a point to remind me. *'You and my daughter will never be.'*

Mal knew I would jump at the chance to be out of Nari's sight.

'It's your choice but, no matter where you run to, your heart will always be here, and it will never feel free.' He was so on point with that one.

What did Luzon want with her? He has no intentions to ransom her – he already knows who I am. What game is he playing?

"Damn it, Nari!" I jump up from my blanket and throw it across the room in frustration. I can't let her remain not when her Father's demise is to take place today.

'Do I allow it?' Do I care one way or another?

That's what I keep asking myself even as I face the rear of the tent that holds Nari imprisoned inside.

It wasn't like she had been treated unjustly but, if she wore another dress that showed off her seductive curves to every Mastion warrior, I would end up gauging their eyes out of their sockets.

'Jealous much?'

I cut open the seam of the tent and slipped inside.

'Nari?' I sent out, hoping that she heard my silent call.

I didn't remember when I could connect with her thoughts but, it was right after I wanted to kiss her; when I told myself that she belonged to me – I belonged to her.

"Zataray?" Nari whirled in my direction and threw herself into my arms. I never wanted to let her go.

"It's alright now, Nari," I soothered her and nodded in the semi-darkened tent and place my hand on my lips.

'Let's get out of here,' I sent.

'It's taken you long enough – you have a whole lot of explaining to do,' Nari sent. I don't even think she realized that she was sending her words into my thoughts.

Our minds linking like this meant that we were, in fact, kindreds. My mom had told me that once. She also mentioned that it was the first connection that indicated to our kind that we would also become mates.

I blinked back the memory of my mom and looked at the princess.

She was dressed and had her dagger out, ready to follow as I led her out the rendered tear I had placed in her holding tent.

"What is this about?" she whispered wanting answers, and not even thanking me for securing her escape.

'You had to go and mess things up, Nari,' I sent. I didn't even understand why my emotions were all over the place, but I made

certain she could keep up. Tears were streaming down her face when I looked back.

Damn. What happened that could break her to the point of tears?

'Stay with me, Nari – the conjuring shield is still in place.' I can feel her follow behind me; she's good at stealth, and I don't worry that she'll fall behind.

I moved away from both camps and out into the jungle area of Borne; it was no easy country for two soldiers on foot without a horse and only a sword and dagger between us.

There's nowhere else I can take her to keep her out of harm's way until the two Kingdoms settle their differences.

"We're going the wrong way," Nari whispered as we took our first breather.

"We can't fight our way through the frontlines where Mal's waiting – the chance of recapture is too great," I replied

"Why did you go to them, Zataray?" she asked.

"Because I was given a choice to do so by your Father and since you 'made' it clear to tell me what you thought of me," I shrugged. " I took the better of the two choices," I said.

"What happened to you?"

I felt hot once more. My core seemed ready to explode like a volcano needing to release its pressure.

My body's temperature continued to elevate by several degrees, and I was irritable as hell. I turned in fury. "You happened, Nari. Your Father and your brother happened. Your people who called me an abomination for being alive happened!"

Nari's eyes are widened; I mean, I think I actually scared her – nothing scared her.

She looked at me as I watched several emotions play across her features – all hinted that I had hurt her.

Nari finally spoke. "If you had only escaped – gone far away."

"Where could I go if your Father wanted to hunt me down – he could do it. The Shamans know everything," I retorted as my anger at the situation grew to the point that my vision displayed everything in crimson.

"Your eyes glow," Nari reeled back – fear etched her face.

I took her by the shoulders to shake her. "You think me a monster too?" I spit on the ground. "That's fine, Nari. You can run back to your people and your father if he still lives after all of this.

"That's cruel," she cried as her voice softened. "I never meant to hurt you, Zataray. I just wanted you to be free and not caught up in any of this," she said.

"I am caught up, Princess!" I said, barely keeping my voice from echoing into the night.

"You can leave me behind now," Nari whispered back; her eyes searched the darkness of Borne and shuddered.

I wasn't certain if she had caught a chill or had been thinking about the creatures that roamed these badlands at night.

'You would not survive without magic,' I sent to her thoughts, and she stiffened in my arms.

"Thank you, your Highness, for reminding me that I 'Broken' as well," Nari whispered as she pushed away from me.

"Damn it, Nari. You always twist my words to fit your view of things – it's not all about you," I growled, realizing that we couldn't even communicate without arguing anymore. "If you rather go back to the Commander?"

"You're jealous?"

"I'm far from it. Like I told you, and you 'informed' me – we will never be together. I don't even like you," I added.

"If you don't like me, why take the risk to rescue me?" Nari asked. Her eyes flared with fire, and I wished at the moment to take her in my arms and roar my desire like the beast she claimed me to be.

"Shut up, Nari," I growled once more. *'It's time to keep moving; follow me.'* And, without a backward glance, I lead us deeper into Borne.

CHAPTER TWELVE – ZATARAY

THE DISTANCE TO FOREVER

It's almost daylight, and we must find a place to stop and rest; I grab a water skin and allow Nari time to catch up before I hand it to her.

"It's not like we can be spotted out in the open with all these trees but, I don't like it – we have to find shelter soon," I retake the water skin and take a drink.

"Will you tell me what the Commander plans? What will happen to our people and its warriors?"

"I'm not certain, Nari," I was supposed to get that information and somehow get it back to Mal but, you came first,"

"I'm sorry – I blew it."

"What's got you so timid?" I asked, observing that ever since we escaped into Borne, Nari hadn't entirely been herself.

"You're changing, Zataray. I've known you for three years – we've pretty much seen each other every day. We know each other better than most – right?"

"Yeah, I guess," I replied.

"Remember your dreams, your Blood-Fire, and now this speaking into my thoughts – is that your half-dragon?"

"I don't have anyone that can tell me one way or the other but, if it is, Nari, that still doesn't mean I can shift – I'm no danger to you," I said as I turned to face her.

Nari's eyes narrowed, and she was right about one thing; I knew her – I even knew what was coming next.

I didn't attempt to avoid her fist into my gut, but damn she could throw a punch.

"Damn it, Nari!" I cursed and grabbed her by the arm to keep her from hitting me again. Her eyes were ablaze, but I was shocked when she burst into tears.

Angry I could handle, but tears? "Hey – wait. Nari? What did I do now – stop it," I said and pulled her into an embrace, holding her while she sobbed her eyes out.

I realized that I had wanted to hold her, and I didn't want our moment together to end.

Nari peered up at me and sniffed. "I'm not afraid of you, Zataray," she whispered. "I love you," she said and sniffed once more.

I stiffened like a board; she always said stuff that shocked me. "That's not what you said in front of your Father and the others," I spoke, almost too quiet for her to hear.

"I couldn't let him find out. Mal warned me – you know what Father's capable of," she explained.

"Yeah, I do. It hurt me, Nari."

"I'm sorry," she said as she looked me in the eyes and placed her hand on my chest. "I don't know how this happened, but I can't take it back."

Nari blushing threw me for a loop; it was the damnedest thing. She was the most amazing girl I had ever known. And at the moment, I felt she was stunning.

"I don't care," I said. "I'm going to let you in on a secret, Nari. I care a lot about you," I said but shook my head no. The time for lies were in the past. "I love you, Nari. I love you so much it feels as if I can never deserve you."

Nari stared into my eyes. "You love me?"

"Even when you drive me crazy," I said with a smile.

Nari blinked as if she was tongued-tied for the first time I had ever known her, and I smiled. "If telling you I love you makes you speechless, maybe I should tell you more often," I teased.

I needed to see her smile again. Yeah, we were in a deep load of trouble, but I could handle a whole army after us if Nari was by my side. "We'll work it out, okay?" I asked.

Nari wiped at her tears, and she never looked more kissable. Instead of kissing her on the lips, I kissed her cheek; I wanted to taste her lips and feel her body next to mine. Times like this when I get these animal instincts to take her; make her mine –I shuddered inside; *'Easy.'*

I pulled away and put away our things as I reached for her hand. "Time to keep moving," I said.

Time sped up, even if it had only been a few turns of the moon since I confessed my love to a crazy, adorable, magicless princess.

I knew things felt different between us, but there was no way I could take back my confession, nor did I want to. I glanced over at Nari and realized she felt the same – we were going to be okay.

I desired Nari, and she loved me – we could make it work.

We were both good, but I knew Luzon had a whole slew of magicians that were just as good or just as fearful of losing their lives if they didn't track us down – they had found us.

"Run," I whispered and grabbed Nari's hand in my own, and we took off at a speed that would make any warrior envious. The thickness of the jungle made it difficult to keep pace, though.

"It's a lot of them," I breathed, attempting to focus on our pursuers. "About a twenty," I surmised.

Nari nodded. "They're loud," she breathed out as well, keeping up with me.

"Nari, I need to tell you something – important," I said.

"It's okay, Zataray – they won't catch us," she assured me.

"It's about your father – the reason he's kept me alive," I replied.

"I know already; you're supposed to help me with my magic –

"No!" I said. I needed her to understand.

I caught the sounds of a waterfall just up ahead and realized where we were. "That's not it, "I said as I changed course and headed for the falls.

The mist created by the falls would allow us some cover.

"It's not that I can't shift, Nari. It's because the Mages are restraining my powers; their magic contains my beast," I confessed.

"They have restrained my abilities since I've come here and continued up until your father gave me the ultimatum to spy on our enemies or they threatened to expose you as Broken," he said.

Nari tugged at my hand. "What are you saying?" she asked.

"That they have been doing the same to you, restraining your magic, and your ability to Magic Wield," I said.

"How do you know this?" Nari stops.

"What are you doing? We have to keep moving," I grab her hand and tug her along toward the water's edge.

"What did they do?"

"Nari, it's magic – they can do anything they want," I say.

"Tell me," Nari tugs her hand from my own, but she didn't slow down and managed to keep up.

"It's – "

My chest felt on fire as a projectile struck me, and I went down to my knees. I coughed blood and looked down.

"Not good," I winced. Our eyes locked. "I'm sorry, Nari," I squeezed out through blood-soaked lips before I coughed once more.

Nari looked down, startled at the arrow that pierced me clean through, its tip protruding from my chest.

'Run, Nari,' I sent to her in hopes I could get through to her, but she wouldn't let go of my hand.

She was stronger than I thought as she pulled me to my feet. "Not without you – I can't," her eyes pleaded with me. "Move it – Dragon boy," she cried.

"You're so beautiful," I whispered as I caressed her cheek. I barely had the strength to lift my arm.

"Tell me later how you really feel later," Nari replied and pulled me toward the falls.

Miraculously, we made it to the edge of the waterfall, but I didn't even have enough strength to draw in a breath; I knew it was the end of the line; I could go no further –

trapped.

"I'm not ever going to stop loving you," I informed her; my chest felt on fire, and my blood burned inside my veins; something was happening to me – my blood boiled.

Tears streamed down Nari's face. "You can't leave me – I won't let you," she cried as she kept her eyes locked with mine.

"You love me, remember – you owe me a kiss," she whispered as tears streamed down her face.

"That's right," I smiled into her eyes. "I do."

Nari shook her head over and over in denial. "I don't care what Father has done; what he tried to do – we are going to be ok."

"Don't cry, Nari. Did I tell you? You were never Broken, your magic is powerful, and it's contained – they're scared of you," I coughed out. I could hear our pursuers approach – too many to escape.

"Stay alive, Nari," I said and pushed her off the edge and into the raging waterfall below.

Laughter ranged out. "All that trouble to hide what you are Half-Blood but, you won't die today – I guarantee it," Luzon hovered over me as he grabbed a handful of my hair; his face lowered to meet my gaze. "The Princess is mine!"

I sensed the darkness close in on me as the Commander's words sank in; my Blood-Fire raged as I struggled to maintain consciousness.

His claim to Nari echoed in the recesses where sanity once thrived but no longer.

I couldn't lift a finger as Luzon gave me the incentive to meet the dark by drawing his knee into my forehead to prove his point.

'Bastard.'

CHAPTER THIRTEEN – NARI

LOST NOT FOUND

A boy with beautiful silver eyes, black curly hair, and bronze skin walked beside me; his eyes caressed me, and I blushed.

'I love you, Nari.'

'I love you too – 'I couldn't remember his name.

I bolted up from lying down, the room still dark from the curtains drawn – it was mid-day.

I yawned. "I slept through the morning again," I admonished my laziness.

I always slept late, and no one dared to disturb me for fear of being reprimanded by my protector.

I couldn't stop yawning either, even as I draped my feet over the bed and committed my body to an all-out stretch.

A knock at the door made me stop my musing as I looked up. "Enter," I replied as a stunning dark-skinned handsome male walked into my bedroom.

His eyes settle on me in a possessive way. "Time to get up, Sleepy-head," Luzon tweaked my nose and smiled.

He was a great guy, and I supposed I had been a real burden on him since these last six months were spent with me, not even remembering a single thing about who I was other than what everyone reminded me of – I was a princess of Avidan.

I caught Luzon staring; he sometimes did that a lot, which made me curious about what he was thinking. We were supposed to be an item.

"Sorry, I can't seem to find energy enough – ever," I apologized.

"You took quite a fall; the Mages did everything just to keep you from death's door. Nari, don't worry; you will recover your vigor and strength in no time," Luzon offered.

"And, my memory?"

"I wanted to show you something if you have the energy to take a ride?"

"Of course, but it's late," I jumped out of bed and walked over to Luzon, and reached up to give him a peck on the cheek. He had been there for me ever since I opened my eyes six months ago. He said I fell from a high place and lost my memory.

Strangely, I didn't even remember my name but, the boy I can see with a perfect memory when he invades my dreams. Who is he? Where is he? Even though I wanted to trust Luzon, I was afraid to ask him anything about my life before my accident.

"Give me a few moments to change into something," I asked.

"Anything for you, Nari," Luzon bowed out of the room and took his leave. "I'll be in the dining room," he said and shut the door.

I took a quick bath and dressed for riding, and when I entered the huge dining area, and couldn't keep the surprise from my voice.

"Wow? What's the occasion?" I asked as I noted the huge spread before us.

"It's just the two of, right?" I asked Luzon.

"Later, other will come but, for now – just us two."

Luzon offered me a seat and helped me place the food that I loved onto my plate. "Thank you," I smiled up into his eyes.

"Anything for you, Nari." I got that Luzon liked me a lot, and I enjoyed his company; I guess I wanted him right back, but there was always a nagging feeling inside my brain that I just couldn't ignore.

Something inside me refused to trust in everything that Luzon did on my behalf. It wasn't as if he was too perfect, but I wanted to stop being so paranoid, whatever it was.

I looked up to find Luzon's eyes on me. There it was again, that feeling. It was what he kept hidden behind his dark eyes, I thought.

Everyone had secrets. Only – I couldn't remember mine.

"Are you ready?" Luzon asked after I pushed my plate away from me; I couldn't eat another bite.

"Of course," I replied and rose to walk by his side.

"You will like this 'surprise,' I think," Luzon said and led us down to the stables. The horses were saddled, and he helped me onto a roan as it nickered.

"It seems he likes you," Luzon suggested and busied himself with his mount before he led us out of the stables.

We began at a good pace, and I followed him without comment; the sun was shining on the horizon, but because it was so late; it was also sinking behind the trees as we entered an area so thick with trees it was difficult to keep the pace or to keep on the path.

"Luzon?" I asked, worried about our destination.

I don't think he even heard me call his name; his eyes were fixed on the road ahead.

"Luzon?" I called once more; he had barely spoken the last two hours. "Where are you taking me?" I asked.

"It's only a little way farther, Nari. The horses won't make it through these trees. Let's unmount; the walk will do you good. You remember the waterfall, don't you?" he asked.

"Walk? Okay – sure. But, I don't remember anything – you know that," I reminded him.

Luzon laughed as if he weren't just the 'moody' guy moments before as he took my hand. "Sure, you do, Nari – it's where I found you after you had been pushed over the edge of the waterfall."

"Pushed?" I stop walking." But, you said I fell."

"Push. Fell. The same thing," Luzon remarked as his eyes held a faraway look. I kept the pace, but barely just because I was fearful that he might drag me down the waterfall if I didn't keep up.

The roar of the magnificent falls was deafening as we approached by way of the valley. I glanced up and noticed the precarious edge that he said I fell from. I shook my head; no way could I have survived that type of fall.

Mist rose around us in an impressive display. I stopped to admire its beauty but, Luzon pulled at my hand, and we followed the path that leads us straight to the bottom of the falls.

"I'm afraid you're going to get wet," Luzon pulled me through with just that slight warning as the raging water cascaded over our heads and fell to meet the pooling waters underneath.

I gasped, shocked by the cold water and by the fact that I had emerged on the other side of the waterfall into what seemed like an oasis.

I attempt to extract the water from my hair and face. "That was so not funny, Luzon," I cried out and whirled to give him a piece of my mind, but I stopped dead in my tracks – we weren't alone.

I blinked at the face that peered back at me; he wasn't someone I'd recognize, I was certain. He looked horrible – like a wild beast.

He didn't move toward us, and then I recognized why as a sheer force type sphere surrounded what appeared to be a tiny island.

Surrounding it was a magnificent pool; another waterfall was centered upon the island and provided the inner part of the pool from the beach area where Luzon and I stood.

I knew immediately that magic was involved and that an impediment spell had contained the mini island – I thought I'd lost him.

A pair of silver eyes bored into my own from across the sphere and blinded me. I stepped into the shallow part of the pool as my tears dripped onto its surface. It was the boy of my dreams – the boy I loved. He looked defeated – almost animalistic.

"Zataray?" I said, dazed.

CHAPTER FOURTEEN – NARI

FOUND, BUT LOST

"Oh, My God," I stared, unable to shift through my returned memories fast enough as I grasp everything all at once.

I whip around; my hands balled into a fist, "Let him go, Luzon!"

"I don't believe you have it right, Princess." Luzon's eyes wandered up to my body and then back down again – I remembered why he made me uneasy.

"What did you do to him," I turn and stare at Zataray; the only genuinely recognizable thing about him had been his eyes – he looked terrible.

"You're alive," I breathe out. "Why did you bring me here, Luzon?" I turned around, unable to hold in my anger; I want to kick his ass, and I pull out my dagger.

"Easy, Princess," Luzon's eyes show his wariness of me. Especially now that I have my memory returned, and I'm more than capable of cutting his throat.

"He won't heal himself. It's been six months, and the mages can't undo what your Father did to him; he is a Half-Blood but, he is still a Shifter, and we need him alive, healthy, and at the peak; of his power."

"So that was your plan before he escaped," I said.

"I knew him to be the Half-Blood, but I also needed him to accept who he was and join us," Luzon continues with his explanation, "That is until I met you."

"Me? I don't understand."

"I knew you possessed a magnificent power, Nari – true you haven't awakened but, the mages were confident that if you were introduced to the right person – "

"The right –

"The man that will make you his wife and seal your power to his own," Luzon said. His suggestion hadn't gone over my head.

"And, you believe I would want that to be you?" I asked incredulously.

"We thought we could force you into making that decision without having to kill you if you didn't join us – me."

"I was with you the whole time – for six months," I added.

"Your power is such that it must be a willing exchange to awaken," Luzon explained.

"And, how did you just decide to show me him," I turned toward Zataray and point in his direction. "What do you take me for really, Luzon? You expect me to be willing after this?" I asked.

"Look at him, Nari. Do you know anything about Shifters? About their Blood-Fire or their power? Did your father ever tell you that when a Dragon Shifter bonds with his mate that they share mind thoughts?"

I turned toward Luzon; certain I couldn't keep the shock from showing on my face.

"So, he has chosen you? Too bad. I meant on keeping you for myself," Luzon sighed; his eyes appeared darker than I ever imagined.

"If he empowers you, I can spare his life – just for you," Luzon said, offering me a bargain.

"Spare him?" I asked, not quite understanding.

"Take a closer look, Nari. Your 'Shifter' barely holds on to thought or life – his Blood-Fire has taken his sanity. If he does not join his mate, that fire will consume him. I'd rather you stayed 'forgetful' a little while longer but, it seems my father is both greedy and impatient; he needs your power and that of your dragon. So, I will leave you two to talk it over," Luzon said and turned to leave.

"You're leaving me?" I asked disbelievingly.

"Neither one of you can breach the containment field but, you can 'Mind-talk,' can't you? See if you can bring him back from his insanity, Nari. See if you can awaken the little boy and not the Dragon," Luzon laughed as he turned his back on me and walked through the back end of the waterfall.

I watched Luzon leave; my mouth was still open, unable to call him back so that I could stab him through his miserable heart.

The silence felt deafening even as the waterfall raged before me, and I turned to face the boy that was no longer a boy inside but a menacing beast.

CHAPTER FIFTEEN – NARI

WHAT AWAKENS

"Zataray?" I spoke his name and settled by the water's edge.

I could feel the pulse of magic that kept us apart, and I could feel the rage inside me as I remember the months that has separated us.

What has happened to Father, Mother, and Mal? Those questions burned inside of me too. But, what was before me also held me to task, and I shook my head, willing myself to focus only on the boy that seemed unaware of my presence.

"Zataray," I called once more. "Don't you remember me?" I asked.

Only I knew what it felt like to be in the dark for so long, unable to remember and lost inside of oneself because of it.

"Luzon says that you're slowly dying – that you won't heal yourself," I spoke as clearly as I could without letting on that I was trembling inside before I remembered that Luzon said I wouldn't be able to break the magic barrier with my voice.

'Zataray,' I sent as I opened my thoughts.

Abilities that weren't mine seemed to surge in a freakish merge that I couldn't even describe as I reached out to touch Zataray's thoughts.

I sensed his rage from here, as well as the animal that ravaged his mind – his sanity barely hung on by a thread.

'Please, Zataray – I love you. Please come back to me,' I begged, waiting for his reaction to my voice – my words.

I felt his resistance, like a black wall that descended to close me off from reaching Zataray's mind.

'Please – please hear me.'

'Princess?'

I tensed as he called me by the name that meant nothing to me.

'I told you, don't call me Princess,' I reprimanded him and tried to keep from jumping with joy. *'Are you okay, Zataray?'*

'He is – gone.'

I jumped to my feet. Did Zataray refer to himself as 'he?' I slowed my breathing and settled into the water; it was shallow and cold.

'I need Zataray to answer me. Luzon says that he is dying – are you the creature that's killing him?' I asked.

It felt bizarre to have this conversation but, I was also fearful of what would become of Zataray if I didn't give it my all – if I didn't try.

I loved him. I couldn't take my eyes off him either, even realizing that he might not love me anymore, believing that I had abandoned him.

'You know me,' I sent. *'We love each other.'*

At least I hoped that this was still the case; it seemed ridiculous really; I had only remembered him five minutes ago. I swallowed deeply to calm my heart from beating out of my chest.

'You left him – '

'You pushed me over a cliff!'

'He is no longer here.'

'I challenge you!' I sent. I didn't even know where the newfound confidence or the strength and knowledge came from, but I knew I must reach my Dragon this way.

I just knew that I had to do something, or like Luzon implied, Zataray would die, and only the creature – the Shifter would remain.

'I accept,' the creature sent.

There was no way in hell I would lose Zataray again, and I reached out and touched my fingers to the magic barrier.

In response, tiny electrical sparks like a shock wave entered my system, but I didn't back down.

The pain intensified and settled into my core but, I didn't give in or release what I had started – I couldn't.

There was someone I was desperate to save, someone I realized that I couldn't live without.

I ignored the increasing pressure that wants to sweep me toward oblivion; in response, I focus only on dropping the barrier as a sudden tingling sensation filters into my being, past my fingertips, and the barrier shattered before me.

"Let's get this over with," I hissed.

I felt impatient and afraid that Luzon would change his mind and drag me away before I could save the boy I loved.

I stepped forward; the water was freezing, and it made my shins ache.

"There's no need to draw this out; you're right," the Shifter's voice carried past the broken barrier.

I expected my challenge answered, but I also sensed that the boy before me wasn't the Zataray I knew and loved.

But one thing was certain; I knew I loved him with all my heart.

My eyes widened when he jumped into the deep end of the pool, leaving his prison behind, and swam toward me in slow, easy strokes.

'Easy now,' I begged my heart to calm its erratic beating.

An indescribable warmth washed through the lower part of my body – Zataray was near.

After all, I began to believe what Luzon told me was true, that some intangible link connected Zataray and me. At first, I thought it had to be Luzon's jealousy talking, but now I wasn't so certain.

A spasm rippled through me, sending white-hot sensations to my core, and something awakened within, but I wasn't ready and slammed the source of it shut.

'Not now.' I knew that I should feel fear.

After all – Zataray's kind was dangerous. My people had spent a century annihilating any that trespassed our kingdom, with my father finally ending the lives of all but one to prove this point.

'I don't want to lose you because you're possibly the last of your kind; I need Zataray though – not you.' I sent because I was afraid to speak as I watched Zataray swim closer.

"Are you certain you wish to go through with this, Princess?" Zataray's voice sent chills down my spine. Still, I lifted my eyes to meet his own.

It was too late to take back my challenge; my chin shot up at the very suggestion that I might lose. *'Never!'*

Zataray swam closer with each stroke of his strong arms; water droplets danced about his magnificent head and shoulders as he glided through the water, barely making a sound.

I remembered the old days when our wordplay formed our bond. "Maybe, it's you...that have second thoughts, Shifter," I swallowed.

My eyes never left his own. While Zataray's eyes seemed to fill with amusement, which makes me angry somehow, I forgot that I was attempting to draw the real Zataray from behind his Shifter persona. He continued to smile at me, and I frowned at his boldness.

"Ah, Princess, you have no sense of humor."

I frowned; his laughter drew forth my desperate need to prove him wrong.

"Zataray, it's okay. I'm here now," I whispered with tears in my eyes, and I blinked them back. He was just a few arm strokes away; even recognizing he wasn't all there, I realized that I loved him fiercely.

Black hair formed around his gorgeous face like wet silk; heavy brows and intense gray eyes locked on to me, and I remembered why I love this boy.

He had my attention alright but, I couldn't ignore the obvious that his thoughts are not his own. What if I lost the challenge? What the heck did I even challenge? I just blurted it out.

My time was up. Zataray rose like a god out of the water to stand before me; I was dumbfounded at how awesome he was and felt oblivious until he laughed – I wanted to slap the smugness right off his face.

'Why do I let him get to me like this?'

We were only an arms width apart, which I decided was way too close, and turned to back out of the water, but Zataray grabbed me by the elbow and pulled my feet out from under me; he dragged me into the deep end of the pool.

"That's very dishonorable of you!" I snapped, forgetting that I was supposed to be saving his Shifter ass from himself.

I hadn't struggled, though. Instead, my mind went to places that had me wondering about my sanity. I was definitely in too deep as it was to feel afraid.

"What are you smiling at, Princess?" The corner of Zataray's eyes narrowed.

I was immensely glad that he couldn't read my thoughts although, I felt uncertain of the bond that Luzon said that Zataray and I both shared – could Zataray read my thoughts too?

Pulled off balance, I fell into Zataray's rough embrace; I felt certain there will be bruising later.

I recognized that it was the Shifter part of Zataray; an almost animalistic desire lurked inside his eyes.

I didn't dare think about the fact that I had placed myself at his mercy – was breaking down the barrier such a clever idea in his weakened state. What If his Dragon controlled him?

Did he want to hurt me? I didn't know.

Zataray hands gripped my elbows, but he had also relaxed his body against mine as we floated together – touching.

He leaned forward. "I'm going to kiss you now, Princess."

"That's not what I'm trying to do here – "I gasped. I could barely keep myself afloat as I panicked. "You can go straight to – "

"Hush, Princess," Zataray whispered; his mouth closed over my own.

'Damn.'

The kiss took my breath away; it wasn't even a gentle kiss. Instead, it demanded I respond.

Zataray's tongue flickered over my lips before entering my mouth; his hand pressed my head forward to meet the demands he placed on me as his other arm wraps possessively around my waist.

'Nari?'

I open my eyes, *'Zataray, oh please – come back to me,'* I plead as tears stream down my face.

Zataray's arms tighten around me, and our bodies surge together where no space, not even water, comes between us as if that were possible.

'I'm here,' he sends. *'I missed you – I love you.'* Heat surges in my belly as his kiss deepens and his words surround me.

'You're back.'

Together we sink toward the bottom of the pool. Only we never make it. I notice the light first as it burst from beneath my fingertips and spreads slowly up my hands, arms, and swirls around my breast before it startles me, taking on a life of its own, stirring agitated – alive.

The light sunk inward to engulf my body; a tingling sensation started downward to my stomach, thighs, and finally my toes – I was aglow.

'Zataray?' I sent in a panic. I didn't know how long I could hold my breath underwater, but Zataray held me in his arms and continued to kiss me silly.

His mouth covered mine, while his lips demanded that I concentrate only on him – focus solely on our bond.

I was burning up.

'It's our joining. The Blood-Fire acknowledges you, Nari. You are mine – I am yours,' he sent.

Zataray hands captured my face; his strong hands held me as if he were afraid to let me go while he breathed into my mouth before he exhaled back out – the transfer was immediate.

I opened my eyes, only to find that I was' breathing unimpeded without any difficulty, underwater.

I also realized that I was still 'glowing.' My eyes gazed into the eyes of the boy who had made it back to me.

Amber eyes stared back – wait. Zataray's eyes were silver-gray – weren't they?

My vision blurred as Zataray began his transformation.

His arms elongated, extending outward until claws took shape where his hands had been; his body stretched and grew as his coloring darkened and black scales appeared where his bronzed skin had been.

An elongated, elegant neck with corded muscles held the most spectacular head of a dragon I had ever seen, with a crest of royal blue and gold near his crown.

'You're beautiful – magnificent,' I sent. Sadness ran through me as I realized what my father had destroyed.

'I am the last of my kind, Princess.' Zataray spoke into my thoughts. *'Our kiss has awakened our gift – the challenge won.'*

For the first time, I could say nothing. I can feel the power coursing through my veins; I can also sense the Dragon that was still within Zataray; it was by no means 'tamed.'

'Something' passed between us – something irrevocable.'

Unfortunately, my assisted breathing only lasted for a few moments as air bubbled escaped, and my lungs decided they needed air, after all, to keep me breathing.

I didn't have time to process it, though, as water surged into my mouth, forcing me upward as I broke the surface. I struggled for a moment, coughing up water, finding my balance, and unable to stop shaking.

The shock of all that has occurred since I woke from my bed this afternoon wore me down.

"Zataray?" I called out in panic. "Zataray!"

I looked for my Dragon but, he was still submerged. I called his name once more. "Zataray?"

Tears stung my eyes. "I didn't know." My voice felt too small – raw.

My dragon emerged, water drenching me as he broke the surface; his wings spread as his words echoed into my thoughts.

'I will always be yours to command, Nari. Your power will have no limits but, my Dragon must eat and rest – I don't know how long I will be gone,' Zataray sent.

"You're leaving me?" I asked.

'Do you believe anyone strong enough to fight you?' Zataray's voice teased me as his laughter fluttered inside my head.

'Call me when you're settled matters – or can't settle matters,' he sent. *'I will always be yours to command, Princess. It shall be so until you release me.'*

"Why would I do that – I'm going to make you pay," I retorted as I placed my hand over my eyes to fight against the glare of the sun as it gleamed off his iridescent black scales.

'Such a feisty princess. When you need me, just think of our kiss – I shall come to you.'

"That's mighty arrogant of you," I sputtered at Zataray's assumption. "I will need you when hell freezes over," I muttered under my breath.

My dragon laughed inside my mind.

"You know what Luzon said, and you're leaving me to face him?" I asked, incredulous that he'd leave me at all after what I had been through.

'You're a big girl. And, I'll be gone only for a little while, Nari – never for long.' Zataray leaped out of the water; his huge wings glistened under the sunlight as he took flight – he was beautiful.

My dragon's amber eyes devoured me. *'I love you, Princess – behave while I'm gone,'* he sent.

And, then he was gone, just like that. Zataray never told me his Dragon name.

'Su ZaTarayn,' Zataray sent to my thoughts; his name seared into my brain; I felt even more connected to him at that moment.

'Find Mal, Nari – he lives.' Zataray's words gave me sweet relief but, he left me to face Luzon, and my body still burned from my dragon's passionate kiss.

"You left me in the deep end!" I yelled.

Zataray's chuckle filtered through my thoughts, and I swam back toward the edge of the waterfall.

Exhausted, my magic yearning to burst forth, along with a new sense of outrage and anger, I clambered out of the water.

Magic burned inside me; I couldn't wait to use it. I glanced about to where I last saw Zataray disappear from my sight in his dragon form.

I hadn't even been conscious of the fact that my fingers touched my swollen lips until my lips tingled, and with it, the surge of power that intensified when I reflected on my dragon – think of our kiss, huh?

A smile lifted the corner of my mouth; I had no more won that challenge than Zataray's Dragon.

My thoughts raced; I had a lot of ground I needed to makeup – things I needed to make right.

My newfound power wouldn't go to waste. I also realized that if my father's death meant anything, it meant that I could now change our people's nomadic thinking.

I could persuade the kingdoms if need be that things were going to change for the better. And Mal was still alive somewhere. I also thought about Luzon and what I am going to do to make him pay.

I wasn't Broken. Finding Zataray once more made me realize that we would find a way to be together somehow. Would we forever change the kingdoms and, in the process, make a better life for those who were treated differently like Zataray and me.

My father once told me that no one should possess such power without first taking on the responsibility it took to understand it properly – by force if necessary.

Zataray loved me; I loved him, and we are about to break down the walls that denounced our humanity and who attempted to dictate to the world that we didn't belong.

My Dragon would return, and with our combined powers, we would attempt to live the happily-ever-after I couldn't envision before.

Let Luzon or his crazy father attempt to stop us. Zataray and I have come to terms with the fact that we belonged to each other as well – this amazed me.

THE END.

ABOUT THE AUTHOR

Gloria Sanders-Williams, aka Desire4Fire, grew up in the San Francisco/Bay Area, where at an early age, her exposure to a creative cultural mix inspired her imagination and writing. She began her writing career at the age of sixteen with works that included short stories and poetry. She recently branched out to evolve her works into a current love of performance poetry at venues throughout the Las Vegas area where she now resides.

"It has become the fruit of my desire to share as a writer works that intrigue through the world of imagination; I hope that I have succeeded — therefore I write."D4F."

#Writemode #IBleedink

THANK YOU

I wrote these 'Shorts' to gain new followings and support, and I hope I've given a little insight into my voice, the voice that desires to be read. There is no greater joy than announcing my dream/vision manifested into the written word. Please accept my invitation to link to my new novel – The Kyandra Saga. I love the genre of Fantasy; the more epic, the better. I hope there's a part of you that enjoys it too. I plan to write for a long time, and with your support on my Go Fund Me page – I believe I can take you to bigger, better worlds full of heroes and life-changing moments. This is my vision. I hope to pass along the dream as I invite you to disregard all you've read about what Fantasy should be and embark upon what I perceive it to become. Join me in these epic adventures. And, I hope you will be pleasantly surprised. I hope you share this work and become a fan yourself, awaiting the upcoming books to fill empty pages. Thank you for your support. Thank you for reading.

Gloria Sanders-Williams aka Desire4Fire

Available now:
http://www.Amazon.com/author/desire4fire
https://www.gofundme.com/-help-fund-my-dream-novel
https://www.Fantasy-author.com

Gloria Sanders-Williams/Desire4Fire c2017
A Desire4Fire Production